What readers a

Michelle, age 14
I think that the Elsie stories are the most wonderful books that I have ever read, apart from the Bible. These books have affected me by helping my faith to grow stronger.

Elizabeth, age 13
The books made me think about how I can live my life for God and that it is possible to have a very strong relationship with him even when you're very young.

Alyssa, age 12
The Elsie books have changed my life! I feel much closer to God! I want to try to be just like Elsie! It has really changed my attitude.

Kelly, age 11
The books helped me get deeper in my faith, and helped me deal with everyday problems. I feel if I didn't have the books, I wouldn't be half as close to God.

Beth, age 10
Ever since I started reading these books I feel like they have inspired me and I have been trying to be like Elsie. I have been going to church forever, but when I sat down and listened I understood it better than I ever did before. I feel like I am finally beginning to relate to the Bible.

Elsie's Endless Wait

Elsie's Endless Wait

BOOK ONE

of the
*A Life of Faith:
Elsie Dinsmore*
Series

Based on the beloved books by
Martha Finley

MCP
Mission City Press

Franklin, Tennessee

Book One of the *A Life of Faith: Elsie Dinsmore* Series

This book is based on the bestselling literary classic *Elsie Dinsmore* written by Martha Finley and first published in 1868 by Dodd, Mead & Company.

Cover & Interior Design: Richmond & Williams, Nashville, Tennessee
Cover Photography: Michelle Grisco Photography, West Covina, California
Interior Typesetting: BookSetters, White House, Tennessee

Special Thanks to Glen Eyrie Castle and Conference Center, Colorado Springs, Colorado, for Photo Shoot Locations

Unless otherwise indicated, all Scripture references are from the Holy Bible, New International Version (NIV). Copyright © 1973, 1978, 1984 by International Bible Society. Used by permission of Zondervan Publishing House, Grand Rapids, MI. All rights reserved.

For more information, write to Mission City Press 202 Second Avenue South, Franklin, Tennessee 37064, or visit our Web Site at **www.alifeoffaith.com**.

For a FREE catalog call 1-800-840-2641.

Library of Congress Catalog Card Number: 99-62804
Finley, Martha
    Elsie's Endless Wait
    Book One of the *A Life of Faith: Elsie Dinsmore* Series
    Hardcover: ISBN-10: 1-928749-01-1
                  ISBN-13: 978-1-928749-01-1
    Softcover: ISBN-10: 1-928749-80-1
                  ISBN-13: 978-1-928749-80-6

Printed in the United States of America
    12 13 14 — 10 09

DEDICATION

This book is
dedicated to
the memory of
MARTHA FINLEY

*May the rich legacy of
pure and simple devotion to Christ
that she introduced through
Elsie Dinsmore in 1868
live on in our day and
in generations to come.*

—FOREWORD—

*I*n this book, the first of the *A Life of Faith: Elsie Dinsmore* Series, you are about to take a trip back in time and to revisit the enduring truths of Christian living. Your journey will begin more than 150 years ago in the American South, two decades before the War Between the States.

At the prosperous plantation of Roselands, you will meet a little girl named Elsie Dinsmore who has never known the love of a parent. You will share Elsie's trials as she deals with resentful and jealous family members, yearns to know and be loved by the father she has never seen, and struggles to find happiness in the face of rejection. From infancy, Elsie has been raised to follow the Bible in every way, including strict observation of the Sabbath, regular prayer and Bible studies, and willing obedience of Jesus' command to love and do good with no expectation of reward. But her unswerving dedication to her Christian principles often causes trouble in the Dinsmore household. With only her loving and faithful nursemaid to rely on, Elsie turns for comfort, guidance, and hope to her little Bible and to Jesus, her closest and truest friend.

Elsie is not perfect by any means, but once you know this extraordinary character, you will find it hard to forget her. So gentle in heart and spirit, yet so strong when the principles of her faith are challenged — Elsie is a nineteenth century child with the power to inspire and uplift people of any era.

Elsie's Endless Wait

Elsie Dinsmore made her first appearance in 1868, and her creator, Martha Finley (1828-1909), eventually wrote twenty-eight novels about the life and times of Elsie. For almost forty years, legions of dedicated readers eagerly welcomed each new Elsie book and treasured them for their enchanting central character and her pure and simple devotion to Christ. But with the arrival of the twentieth century, the popularity of the series faded, and Elsie was nearly forgotten. Now, almost a century after Miss Finley's death, interest in the adventures of her charming Christian heroine has been revived.

Mission City Press is very proud to continue Miss Finley's commitment to Christian faith and the Christian heart by re-introducing Elsie Dinsmore for a new generation and generations to come. It is our hope that you will not only enjoy every one of Elsie's adventures but will also find in them, as we have, a source of spiritual inspiration that is ageless.

This version is a careful adaptation of the *Elsie Dinsmore* series, faithful to the original yet rewritten for modern readers. Since every effort has been made to preserve the nineteenth century flavor of Miss Finley's original text, some terms and customs may require explanation and historical context. The following brief overview of some of the differences between Elsie's era and modern times will, it is hoped, add to the reader's appreciation of the story.

∾ WELCOME TO ELSIE'S WORLD ∾

In the 1830s, when Elsie was born, the family was the fundamental unit of society, just as it is now, but couples married at earlier ages and large families were common.

Foreword

Several generations often lived together, and members of a single household might include grandparents and great-grandparents, aunts, uncles, and cousins as well as immediate family. Children were expected to respect the full authority of their parents and to obey all their elders.

Life expectancy was much shorter than it is today. Because medical knowledge was limited and modern methods of treatment such as antibiotics had not been discovered, virtually every illness in a family was regarded as a serious threat. Childhood diseases that are easily prevented or cured today were especially feared by parents in the nineteenth century.

Apart from trains and steamboats, there were no motorized forms of transportation in Elsie's day, and few paved roads outside large cities. People depended on horses, carriages, and their own feet to take them from place to place. Schools were scarce in the rural South, and children were usually educated at home; wealthy families frequently employed live-in governesses to teach, although teenage boys were sometimes sent to boarding schools. Children learned many of their lessons by rote, or exact memorization, and perfection was expected in their oral recitations of these daily assignments. Even very young children memorized lengthy Biblical passages. This explains Elsie's ability to quote the Scriptures. The Bible was an important part of the total educational process in many families. It was used to teach spelling, grammar, and composition, as well as lessons in morality and proper conduct.

In the 1800s, people had no radios or televisions, no films or videos or audio recordings, no computers and no telephones. In this era, reading and letter-writing were the primary media for communicating news, entertainment, and learning. Letter-writing was considered an art,

newspapers flourished, and books were prized posses-
sions even in the poorest homes. Visiting was also an
important means of bridging the great distances between
isolated farms and plantations. Wealthy homes were often
full of guests whose stays extended from overnight to
days, weeks, even months. In our story, friends and business associates join the Dinsmore family at mealtime, and
in the Old South (indeed, in many parts of the South
today), the main meal of the day, served at noon or one
o'clock, was called "dinner." The lighter evening meal was
"supper."

The Dinsmores are fortunate to live near a church
which they can attend each week. But in more remote
areas, Christian worship was observed at home, and families welcomed the occasional visit of clergymen, sometimes called "circuit riders," who traveled the countryside
on horseback. Plantation-owners were expected to attend
to the spiritual needs of their slaves and sometimes
employed clergy to conduct services.

At the time this book begins, slavery was an accepted
economic and social reality in the Antebellum South. Well-
to-do planters with large estates, such as the senior Mr.
Horace Dinsmore, "owned" many African-American slaves
who were regarded as private property. The workers who
plowed and planted and harvested the crops were the "field
slaves," while "house servants" tended to the needs of the
owner, his family, and the large plantation houses.

A master could do much as he pleased to discipline his
slaves and could sell his slaves at any time, often separating
families in the process. Although the planter's control was
nearly absolute, the law regulated the master-slave relationship to some extent. For example, it was illegal to teach

a slave to read and write, so the character of Aunt Chloe, who is Elsie's nursemaid, possesses a knowledge of Scripture learned by memorizing what she heard from Christian masters.

While many Southerners and Southern churches abhorred slavery and sought to abolish its practice, the right to own slaves was not officially ended in all the United States until the 1865 ratification of the Thirteenth Amendment to the Constitution.

Although Martha Finley wrote about the South, she never lived in the region or experienced slavery directly. She did, however, hold a firm belief in the importance of unity and equality among all people and all parts of her native land, and she wrote poignantly, in the preface to a later Elsie book, of "this great, grand, glorious old Union . . . . " She issued a plea to her readers and fellow countrymen to "forget all bitterness, and live henceforth in love, harmony, and mutual helpfulness."

DINSMORE FAMILY TREE

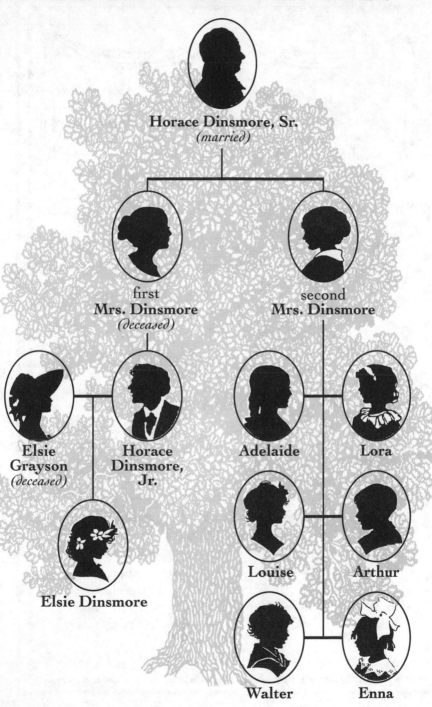

Horace Dinsmore, Sr.
(married)

first
Mrs. Dinsmore
(deceased)

second
Mrs. Dinsmore

**Elsie
Grayson**
(deceased)

**Horace
Dinsmore,
Jr.**

Adelaide

Lora

Elsie Dinsmore

Louise

Arthur

Walter

Enna

Roselands, a cotton plantation near a coastal city in the Old South during the early 1840s, some years prior to the American Civil War and the abolition of slavery.

CHARACTERS

∽ The Dinsmore Household ∽

Mr. Horace Dinsmore, Sr. — The owner and master of Roselands plantation; Elsie's grandfather.

Mrs. Dinsmore — Mr. Dinsmore's second wife and mother of six children:

Adelaide — Age 16	**Lora** — Age 14
Louise — Age 12	**Arthur** — Age 10
Walter — Age 8	**Enna** — Age 6

Mr. Horace Dinsmore, Jr. — Age 26: The only son of Horace Dinsmore, Sr., and his first wife, who died when Horace was a small boy. Once married to Elsie Grayson of New Orleans, Horace is a lawyer by training.

Elsie Dinsmore — Age 8: The daughter of Horace Dinsmore, Jr., and Elsie Grayson, who died shortly after Elsie's birth. Born in New Orleans, Elsie has lived at Roselands since she was four years old.

Miss Rose Allison — Age 17: Daughter of the Allisons of Philadelphia. She visits Roselands and becomes a close friend of Adelaide Dinsmore and Elsie.

Mrs. Murray — A Scots Presbyterian woman of deep Christian faith. Mrs. Murray was housekeeper to Elsie's guardian in New Orleans. She accompanied Elsie to Roselands but is now living in her native Scotland.

Miss Day — The children's teacher.

Slaves of Roselands Plantation

Aunt Chloe — The middle-aged nursemaid who has cared for Elsie since birth and taught her in the Christian faith.

Pompey — The chief house servant at Roselands and a special friend of Elsie's.

Jim — A young slave who works in the stables and frequently "babysits" the young Dinsmore children during their outings.

Aunt Phoebe — The Roselands cook and mother of Jim.

Ajax — An expert horseman and the Roselands carriage driver.

Fanny — A chambermaid.

The Travillas of Ion Plantation

Edward Travilla — Owner of Ion and friend since boyhood of Horace Dinsmore, Jr.

Mrs. Travilla — Widowed mother of Edward, dedicated Christian, and caring friend to Elsie.

The Carringtons of Ashlands Plantation

Mr. and Mrs. Carrington — Old friends of the Dinsmore family, owners of Ashlands plantation, and parents of five children including:

Lucy and Herbert — Age 8, twin sister and brother; Elsie's playmates.

CHAPTER 1

Trouble in the Schoolroom

*"It is better, if it is God's will,
to suffer for doing good
than for doing evil."*

1 PETER 3:17

The schoolroom at Roselands was a very pleasant room. True, its ceiling was lower than in the rest of the large plantation house. But the schoolroom was in the wing built in the days before the Revolutionary War, while the main portion of the house was not more than thirty years old. The effect of the low ceiling was offset by tall windows that reached to the floor and opened onto a sunny veranda. The veranda overlooked a lovely flower garden, and the vista beyond offered shade trees, thick woods, and acre upon acre of farm fields. In this rich Southern earth, cotton was grown and picked to be shipped to mills in all parts of the world.

Roselands was the estate of Mr. Horace Dinsmore, Sr., and his house — surrounded by its many outbuildings, stables, gardens, orchards and, at a distance, the living quarters of the slaves — was the hub of all activity on the vast plantation.

On the warm, fall morning when this story begins, the activity in the Roselands schoolroom included lessons in history and geography, English literature and French grammar, arithmetic and penmanship. Six Dinsmore children of varying ages labored at their neat rosewood desks under the sharp eye and quick tongue of Miss Day, the governess.

Miss Day was giving a lesson to six-year-old Enna, the youngest of the group, and Miss Day's patience was wearing thin. The spoiled pet of both her father and her mother, Enna was a willful girl who often pushed her teacher to the limits.

3

"There!" exclaimed Miss Day as she shut the book and impatiently tossed it onto the desk. "I might as well try to teach old Bruno, for your dog would learn about as fast as you, Enna."

With a pout on her pretty face, Enna walked away, muttering under her breath that she would "tell Mamma."

Looking at her watch, Miss Day announced, "Young ladies and gentlemen, I will leave you to your studies for an hour. Then I will return to hear your recitations. Those of you who have done your work properly will be permitted to ride with me to the fair this afternoon."

"Oh, that will be jolly!" exclaimed Arthur, a bright ten-year-old with a love of mischief.

"Hush!" Miss Day said sternly. "I don't want to hear any more outbursts from you, Arthur. And remember, you won't go to the fair unless you have learned your lessons thoroughly."

Looking to Louise, who was twelve, and fourteen-year-old Lora, Miss Day instructed, "Girls, your French lessons must be perfect, and your English lessons as well."

Alone at a desk near one of the windows, a little girl of eight was bent over her slate and gave every appearance of industry. To her, Miss Day barked, "Elsie, every figure of that arithmetic problem must be correct, and your geography lesson must be recited perfectly, and you must write a page in your copybook without a single blot of ink."

"Yes, ma'am," the girl replied meekly. For an instant, Elsie raised her soft hazel eyes to her teacher, then immediately dropped her gaze back to the numbers chalked on her slate writing tablet.

Miss Day issued her final command to a shy boy of eight who was working quietly at his desk: "Walter, if you miss

one word of your spelling, you will stay at home and learn the whole lesson again. And all of you are to remain in this room until I return."

"Unless Mamma interferes, as she's sure to do," Arthur said in a low voice as Miss Day's quick steps retreated down the hall.

For perhaps ten minutes, all was quiet in the schoolroom. Each child seemed absorbed in study until Arthur jumped up and threw his book across the room.

"I know my lessons," he exclaimed, "and even if I didn't, I wouldn't study another bit for old Day — or Night, either!"

"Do be quiet, Arthur," his sister Louise begged. "I can't study when you make so much racket."

Silenced, Arthur tiptoed across the room and crept up behind Elsie. Taking a feather from his pocket, he tickled it at the back of her neck. She jumped in surprise, then pleaded with Arthur to stop.

"But it pleases me to bother you," Arthur said, and he tickled her once more.

With all the persuasion she could muster, Elsie asked him again, "Please leave me alone, or I'll never get this problem done."

"All this time on one little problem?" Arthur replied with a sneering laugh. "You ought to be ashamed, Elsie Dinsmore. Why, I could have done it a half a dozen times before now."

"Well, I've been over it and over it," Elsie said sadly, "and there are still two numbers that won't come out right."

"How do you know they're not right, little miss?" Arthur asked, grabbing at her curls as he spoke.

5

"Please don't pull my hair!" she cried. Then she explained that she had the correct answer, so she knew that her answer was wrong.

"Then why not just write down the right numbers?" Arthur asked. "That's what I'd do."

"But that wouldn't be honest."

"Nonsense! Nobody will know if you cheat a little."

"It would be like telling a lie," Elsie said firmly, then sighed and put aside her slate. "But I'll never get it right with you bothering me."

Elsie tried to turn her attention to her geography book, but Arthur would not stop his persecutions. He tickled her, pulled at her hair, flipped the book out of her hands, and kept up his incessant chatter and questions. On the verge of tears, Elsie begged him once again to leave her to her lessons.

"Take your book out on the veranda, Elsie, and study there," said Louise. "I'll call you when Miss Day comes back."

But Elsie did not budge from her desk. "I can't go outside because Miss Day said we must stay in this room, so that would be disobeying," she explained with despair.

Giving up on the geography, she took her copybook and pen and ink from her desk. She dipped her pen into the ink and very carefully formed every letter on the clean, white paper. But Arthur stood over her as she wrote, criticizing every letter she made. At last, he jogged her elbow, and all the ink in her pen dropped onto the paper, making a large black blot.

It was too much, and Elsie burst into tears. "Now I won't get to ride to the fair! Miss Day will never let me go! And I wanted so much to see the beautiful flowers."

Arthur, who was not always as hateful as he seemed, felt suddenly guilty about the mischief he had caused. "Never mind, Elsie. I can fix it," he said. "I'll just tear out this page with the ink stain, and you can start again on the next page. I won't bother you anymore, and I can help with your arithmetic problem, too."

Elsie smiled at him through her tears. "That's kind of you, Arthur, but I can't tear out the page or let you do my problem. That would be deceitful."

Arthur didn't expect his offer to be refused. He drew himself up and tossed his head. "Very well, little miss," he said with his usual smugness. "If you won't let me help, then it's your own fault if you have to stay home."

Louise was also astounded. "Elsie, I have no patience with you," the older girl exclaimed. "You always raise such ridiculous scruples. I won't pity you at all if you have to stay home."

Elsie said nothing. Brushing away her tears, she returned to her writing, and though she took great pains with every letter, she thought sadly, "It's no use. That ugly ink blot spoils it all."

When she finally finished the page, it looked very neat except for the blot. Then she returned to the arithmetic problem on her slate. Patiently, she went over every number, trying to find her mistake. But there was not enough time left, and she was so upset by Arthur's teasing that she couldn't concentrate on the work.

The hour was up, and Miss Day returned. Still, Elsie thought she might be able to complete her assignments, if only Miss Day would call on the other children first. Perhaps Arthur would explain about the ink blot, and everything would be alright after all.

Elsie's Endless Wait

As soon as the teacher had taken her seat, however, she called, "Elsie, come here. Bring your book and recite your geography lesson for me, and I want to see your copybook and your slate."

Although trembling with fear, Elsie recited quite well, for she had studied her geography before coming to the schoolroom that morning. But her recitation was not perfect, and with a frown, the teacher handed back the textbook. Miss Day was always more severe with Elsie than any of her other pupils — for reasons that will soon become clear.

Noting the two incorrect numbers in Elsie's arithmetic problem, Miss Day put down the girl's slate and opened the copybook. "You careless, disobedient child!" she shouted. "Didn't I tell you not to blot your book? There will be no ride for you today. You have failed in everything. Go back to your seat! Correct that problem and do the next one. Then write another page in your copybook. And mind, if there is a blot on the page, you will not get your dinner today!"

Arthur, who pretended to be studying at his desk, had watched Elsie throughout this scene, and his conscience clearly troubled him. But when Elsie looked at him imploringly as she returned to her desk, he turned his face away and whispered to himself, "It's her own fault. She wouldn't let me help, so it's her own fault."

Glancing up again, he saw that his sister Lora was staring at him, and her eyes blazed with scorn and contempt.

"Miss Day," Lora said indignantly, "since Arthur won't speak up, I have to tell you that it's all his fault that Elsie failed her lessons. She tried her very best, but he was teasing her constantly, and he also made her spill the ink on her copybook. She was too honorable to tear out the page or let him do her arithmetic, which he said he would do."

Trouble in the Schoolroom

"Is this so, Arthur?" Miss Day demanded angrily.

The boy hung his head but didn't reply.

"Alright then," Miss Day said, "you will stay at home as well."

Lora was amazed. "Surely you won't punish Elsie now that I've told you it wasn't her fault."

Miss Day only turned her haughty gaze on Lora, and with ice in her voice, she said, "Understand this, Miss Lora. I will not be dictated to by any of my pupils."

Lora bit her lip, but she said nothing more.

As the other children recited their lessons, Elsie sat at her desk and struggled with the feelings of anger and indignation that were boiling inside her. Although she possessed a gentle and quiet spirit, Elsie was not perfect, and she often had to do fierce battle with her naturally quick temper. But because she seldom displayed her anger to others, it was commonly said within the family that Elsie had no spirit.

The other children had just finished their lessons when the door opened and a tall woman dressed in elegant riding clothes entered the schoolroom.

"Through yet, Miss Day?" Mrs. Dinsmore asked.

"Yes, madam, we are just done."

"Well, I hope your pupils have all done well and are ready to accompany us on the ride to the fair." Perhaps it was the sound of Elsie's sniffling that attracted Mrs. Dinsmore's attention at that moment. "What is the matter with Elsie?" she inquired of the teacher.

"She failed in all her lessons, and I've told her that she must stay home today," Miss Day replied, her anger rising again. "And since Miss Lora tells me that Arthur was partly to blame, I've forbidden him to come with us, too."

"Excuse me for correcting you," Lora said indignantly to her teacher. "I did not say 'partly,' because I'm sure it was *entirely* Arthur's fault."

Miss Day didn't have a chance to reply, as Mrs. Dinsmore addressed her daughter curtly, "Hush, Lora. How can you be sure of such a thing? Miss Day, I must beg you to excuse Arthur this time, for I have my heart set on his coming with us today. He's mischievous, I know, but he's just a child, and you shouldn't be too hard on him."

Miss Day's back stiffened, but she spoke with strained courtesy: "Very well, madam. You, of course, have the right to control your own children."

As Mrs. Dinsmore turned to leave, Lora spoke up again: "Mamma, won't Elsie be allowed to go?"

"Elsie is not my child, and I have nothing to say about it," Mrs. Dinsmore said with a condescending air. "Miss Day knows all the circumstances, and she is better able than I to decide whether Elsie deserves her punishment."

When her mother had gone, Lora turned to the teacher. "You will let Elsie go, won't you, Miss Day?"

Her anger now doubled by the insult from Mrs. Dinsmore, Miss Day replied, "I've already told you, Miss Lora, that I will not be dictated to. I've said that Elsie must stay at home, and I will not break my word."

"Why do you concern yourself with Elsie's troubles?" Louise whispered to her sister as Lora returned to her seat. "Elsie is so full of silly principles that I have no pity for her."

Meanwhile, Miss Day had crossed the room to stand over Elsie's desk. "Didn't I tell you to learn that lesson over?" the teacher asked. "Why are you sitting here doing nothing?"

The little girl held her head in her hands as she fought to overcome her feelings. She didn't dare to speak because her anger might show in her words, so she brushed at her tears and opened her book. But Miss Day would not be satisfied. She was angry too, at Mrs. Dinsmore's interference and at the knowledge that she herself was acting unfairly. But Miss Day, unlike Elsie, could not keep her anger hidden. She was determined to vent her displeasure, and Elsie was, as usual, her innocent target.

"Why don't you speak?" Miss Day demanded, and she grabbed Elsie by the arm and shook the girl roughly. "Answer me this instant! Why have you been idling all morning, you lazy girl?"

"I haven't been idling," Elsie protested quickly. "I tried hard to do my work, and you're punishing me when I don't deserve it."

"How dare you? There!" Miss Day shouted, smacking Elsie hard on the ear. "Take that for your impertinence!"

Elsie wanted to shout her own harsh reply, but she restrained herself. Looking at her book, she tried to study, but her ear ached painfully and hot tears came so fast that she could not see the page.

It was at that moment that one of the house servants came to the door and announced that the carriage was ready, and Miss Day, followed by Lora, Louise, and the younger children, hurried from the schoolroom. Elsie, at last, was alone.

Putting aside her geography book, she opened her desk and took out her pocket Bible. The little book showed all the marks of frequent use. Elsie turned its pages deliberately and soon found the passage she sought. Fighting back her tears, she read to herself:

"'For it is commendable if a man bears up under the pain of unjust suffering because he is conscious of God. But how is it to your credit if you receive a beating for doing wrong and endure it? But if you suffer for doing good and you endure it, this is commendable before God. To this you were called, because Christ suffered for you, leaving you an example, that you should follow in His steps.'"

Now her tears came again. "I haven't done it," she sobbed, "I didn't endure it. I'm afraid I'm not following in His steps very well."

"My dear child, what is the matter?" asked a gentle voice, and a soft hand was laid on Elsie's shoulder.

The little girl looked up into the pleasant face of a young woman. "Miss Allison!" Elsie said in surprise. "I thought I was all alone."

"You were, my dear, till this moment," soothed Rose Allison, a recently arrived guest in the Dinsmore home. She drew up a chair and sat close beside Elsie. "I was on the veranda when I heard sobbing, and I came in to see if I could help. Won't you tell me the cause of your distress?"

The young woman's voice was full of kindness, but Elsie couldn't answer; her tears choked her and made speaking impossible.

So Rose went on, "I think I understand. Everyone has gone to the fair, and they've left you at home. Perhaps you have to memorize a lesson that you failed to recite."

The young woman's sweet voice and touch calmed Elsie a little, and she was able to answer, "Yes, ma'am, but being left is not the worst." Then her voice failed her again, and she could only point to the words she had been reading in her Bible.

With a fresh burst of tears, she sobbed out her misery. "I — I didn't do it! I didn't bear it patiently. They weren't fair, and I was punished when I wasn't to blame. Then I — I got angry. I'm afraid that I'll never be like Jesus. Never!"

Rose Allison, who had been at Roselands for just a few days, was extremely surprised by the child's great emotion. A devoted Christian herself, Rose was pained by the Dinsmore family's apparent disregard for the teachings of God's Word. She hadn't known the family before her visit, but her father was an old friend of Mr. Dinsmore's. As a kindness, Mr. Dinsmore had prevailed on Mr. Allison to allow Rose, who had been ill that year, to travel from her home in Philadelphia. She was spending the winter at Roselands where she could regain her strength in the warmth of the Southern climate. Although she was enjoying her visit and feeling much better, she had been struck by the family's lack of devotion. But until now, she had not spoken with Elsie.

Rose wrapped her arm around the child's waist. "My poor Elsie," she said. "That is your name, isn't it?"

"Yes, ma'am. Elsie Dinsmore."

"Well, Elsie, as you probably know, becoming like Jesus is the work of a lifetime, and we all stumble along the way. But Jesus understands, dear."

"Yes ma'am," Elsie said. "I know He does, but I'm so sorry that I've grieved Him and displeased Him. I do love Him, and I want so much to be like Him."

Rose stroked Elsie's hair and spoke tenderly, "But remember Elsie, God's love for us is *far* greater than we could ever imagine and it doesn't depend on our goodness, because none of us can be good enough on our own. It is

Jesus' righteousness that is credited to our account. You must have patience, little one. His Holy Spirit in you will bring about the purity of heart you desire."

Elsie was silent for a few moments as she thought about what the young woman had said. Then she brightened. "Thank you, Miss Allison," she said sincerely.

"And thank you, Elsie," Rose said with a little laugh, "for I'm very glad to find another person in this place who loves Jesus and is trying to do His will. I love Him too, so we will love each other."

Elsie was overjoyed. "Oh, I'm so glad," she said, "for no one loves me but my Aunt Chloe."

"Who is that?" Rose asked.

"My nursemaid," Elsie replied. "Aunt Chloe has always taken care of me. Have you seen her in the house?"

Rose considered. "Perhaps," she said thoughtfully. "I've met a number of nice servant women since I came here. But tell me, Elsie, who taught you about Jesus, and how long have you loved Him?"

"Ever since I can remember," Elsie said. "It was Aunt Chloe who told me how He suffered and died on the cross for us. She talked to me about Him just as soon as I was old enough to understand. Then she'd tell me about my own mother and how she loved Jesus and had gone to be with Him in heaven when I was just a week old. When my mother was dying, she put me into Chloe's arms and said, 'Take my dear baby and love her and care for her just as you did me. And be sure to teach her to love God.'"

Elsie drew from the bodice of her dress a gold chain from which hung a miniature portrait set in a golden locket. It was the picture of a beautiful young girl, no more than fifteen or sixteen years old. She had the same hazel eyes and brown curls that Elsie possessed, and the same regular features, fine complexion, and sweet smile.

"This is my mother," Elsie said softly as she placed the miniature in Rose's hand.

The young woman gazed at the portrait admiringly, then she turned to Elsie in puzzlement. "I don't understand," Rose said. "Are you not the sister of Enna and the other children? Is Mrs. Dinsmore not your mother?"

"She is their mother, but not mine," Elsie replied. "My father, Horace Dinsmore, Jr., is their brother, so all the other children are my aunts and uncles."

"Indeed," Rose mused. "And your father is away, isn't he?"

"Yes, ma'am. He's in Europe. He has been away since before I was born, and I've never seen him. Oh, I do wish he'd come home! I want to see him so much! Do you think he would love me, Miss Allison? Do you think he would put me on his knee and hug me the way Grandpa hugs Enna?"

"I'm sure he would, my dear. How could he help loving his own little girl?" said Rose, and she gently kissed Elsie's cheek.

Then she stood, picking up the little Bible and turning its pages. "I must go now and let you learn your lesson," she said. "But perhaps you'd like to come to my room in the mornings and evenings and read your Bible to me."

"Oh, yes, ma'am," Elsie exclaimed, and her eyes sparkled with delight. "I love reading the Bible best of anything! Aunt Chloe has always taught me that I must 'hide the Word in my heart.'"

"And have you memorized all of your verses by heart?" Rose inquired.

"Not all of them," Elsie said honestly. "But I've memorized many beautiful passages."

"Can you recite something for me?" Rose asked, for she could see that their discussion of God's Word greatly cheered the child.

Elsie thought for a few moments, then said: "Yes, ma'am. These verses from Colossians are some of my favorites." She quoted carefully: "'Therefore, as God's chosen people, holy and dearly loved, clothe yourselves with compassion, kindness, humility, gentleness and patience. Bear with each other and forgive whatever grievances you may have against one another. Forgive as the Lord forgave you. And over all these virtues put on love, which binds them all together in perfect unity.'"

"That is excellent, Elsie!" Rose said, smiling brightly. "And why do you like those verses?"

"Because they're so clear to me, Miss Allison. I sometimes have trouble understanding what I read in the Scriptures."

"Then perhaps I can help you. If you like, we can study God's Word together," Rose said.

"Oh, how kind you are," Elsie replied happily. "I would like that very much."

"Then please come and visit with me this evening," Rose said, and putting the little Bible into the child's hand, she kissed Elsie once again before she left.

Returning to her own room, Rose found Adelaide Dinsmore, the eldest of the Dinsmore daughters. Adelaide was nearly Rose's age, and the two young women had become

friends. Now she was seated on the sofa and working busily on some embroidery.

"I'm glad to see that you're making yourself at home," Adelaide said as Rose entered. "Where have you been for so long?"

"I was in the schoolroom, talking with little Elsie. I thought she was your sister, but she tells me she is not."

"No, she's my brother Horace's child," Adelaide replied. "I thought you knew, but since you don't, I may as well tell you the whole story.

"Horace was a wild boy, pampered and spoiled and used to having his own way. When he was seventeen, he insisted on going to New Orleans to spend some time with a school-mate. While he was there, he met a very beautiful girl and fell desperately in love with her. Her name was Elsie Grayson, and she was a year or two younger than he — an orphan and very wealthy. Horace knew that the families would object to their marrying because of their ages, so he persuaded the girl to elope and marry in secret. They had been married for several months before any of their friends suspected it."

Adelaide paused to thread a new strand of silk through her needle; then she continued her story: "When the news finally reached Papa, well, you can imagine how angry he was, and only in part because Horace and his bride were so young. You see, old Mr. Grayson was a tradesman and had made all his money in business, so my father didn't consider the daughter to be quite my brother's equal. Papa made Horace come home and then sent him away to college in the North. My brother studied law, and he's been traveling abroad ever since."

"But what about his wife?" Rose asked. "Elsie's mother?"

"I was just coming to her," said Adelaide. "Since her parents were dead, she had a guardian, and he was just as opposed to the marriage as Papa was. She was made to believe that Horace would never return to her. All his letters were intercepted, and finally she was told that he had died. As Aunt Chloe says, the girl 'grew thin and pale and weak and melancholy,' and she died when little Elsie wasn't quite a week old.

"We'd never met Horace's wife, and when she died, it seemed right that little Elsie stay on in the guardian's house. She was cared for by Aunt Chloe, who had been her mother's nursemaid, and by the housekeeper there, a Scotswoman named Mrs. Murray."

Adelaide looked up from her embroidery, and Rose could see that her face had become serious. "It was about four years ago that the guardian died," Adelaide continued, "and little Elsie, Aunt Chloe, and Mrs. Murray came to live with us. Horace never comes home, and he doesn't seem to care for his child. He never mentions her in his letters except in connection with business affairs. He's never even seen Elsie. Of course, I haven't spoken to my brother in many years, but I believe he must associate his child with the loss of his wife, for he did love Elsie's mother with all his heart. Perhaps that is the reason he has stayed away from his daughter."

"But she's such a dear little girl," Rose said. "I'm sure he'd love her if he could only meet her."

"Yes," Adelaide agreed, "she is dear enough, and I often feel sorry for her loneliness. When she came here, you see, she had never been around other children, and it has been difficult for her. I must admit that my brothers and sisters have not always been welcoming, but the truth is, I think we

are all a little jealous of her. You've seen that she's very beautiful, and she is also heiress to an immense fortune. I have often heard Mamma fret that someday Elsie will quite eclipse my younger sisters."

Rose was confused by Adelaide's last statement. "Why would your mother feel jealous, " she asked, "when little Elsie is her own granddaughter?"

"But that's not the case," Adelaide explained, "for Horace is not my mother's son. His own mother died when he was quite young, and he was seven or eight when my mother married Papa, and" — she lowered her voice and her eyes — "I don't believe Mamma was ever very fond of him."

Both young women sat quietly for several minutes as Rose pondered this new information. "No wonder the little girl longs so for her father's love," she thought to herself, "and carries such grief for the mother she never knew." Adelaide's recounting of Elsie's lonely birth and her sad position among the Dinsmores perhaps explained, as well, the unusual maturity that Rose had sensed in the child. "God," Rose thought, "may be her only true friend."

At last Adelaide spoke again. "Elsie is an odd child, and I don't really understand her. She is so meek and patient that she will virtually allow the other children to trample her. Her meekness provokes my Papa, and he says she is no Dinsmore because she doesn't know how to stand up for herself. Yet Elsie does have a temper, I know. Ever so often it shows itself, but just for an instant. Then she grieves over it as if she had committed some crime, whereas the rest of us think nothing of getting angry a dozen times a day. And then she is always poring over that little Bible of hers, though what she finds so interesting I can't say. To me, it's the dullest of books."

"How strange," Rose said in surprise. "I'd rather give up all other books than the Bible. The Word of God is more precious to me than gold!"

Now it was Adelaide's turn to be astonished. "Do you *really* love the Bible so? Will you tell me why?"

"For its great and precious promises, Adelaide, and for its teachings about holy living. It offers inner peace and pardon from sin and eternal life," Rose said. "The Bible brings me the glad news of salvation offered as a free, unmerited gift. It tells me that Jesus died to save sinners such as me and that through Him, I am reconciled to God."

Adelaide could hear the deep emotion in her friend's voice as Rose went on, "I often find that my feelings and thoughts are not what they should be, and the blessed Bible tells me how my heart and mind can be renewed. When I find myself utterly unable to keep God's holy law, the Bible tells me of One who kept it for me, and who willingly suffered for my sins," Rose said with a solemn passion that made her seem much older than her seventeen years.

Both women sat silently for a time. Then Adelaide's face clouded, and she said a little sternly, "You talk as if you were a great sinner, Rose, but I don't believe it. It's only your humility that makes you think like that. Why, what have you ever done? If you were a thief or a murderer or guilty of some terrible crime, I could understand your saying such things about yourself. Excuse me for this, Rose, but your language seems absurd for a refined, intelligent, and amiable young lady."

Gently, Rose responded to her friend's complaint. "'Man looks at the outward appearance, but God looks at the heart,'" she quoted. Then she explained, "From my earliest existence, God has required the undivided love of my whole heart, soul, strength, and mind; yet until the last two years,

I was in rebellion against Him, not allowing Him to govern my life. For all my life, He has showered blessings on me. He has given me life and health, strength and friends — everything necessary for happiness. But I gave back nothing but ingratitude and rebellion. All that time I rejected His offers of pardon and reconciliation and resisted all the efforts of God's Holy Spirit to draw me to Him."

Rose's voice quivered, and her eyes brimmed with tears. "Can you not now see me as a sinner?"

Adelaide moved closer to her friend's side and put her arm around Rose's shoulders. "Don't think of these things, dear Rose," she gently admonished. "Religion is too gloomy for one as young as you."

"True religion is not gloomy at all," Rose answered, hugging Adelaide in return. "I never knew what true happiness was until I found Jesus. My sins often make me sad, but my faith in Him? Never."

CHAPTER

2

Someone To Talk To

*"The purposes of a man's heart
are deep waters, but a man
of understanding draws
them out."*

PROVERBS 20:5

When Rose Allison had left the schoolroom, Elsie got up from her desk and knelt down with her Bible before her. In her own simple words, she poured out her story to the dear Savior she loved so well, confessing that when she had done right and suffered for it, she had not endured the injustice. Earnestly, she prayed to be made like the meek and lowly Jesus, and as she prayed, her tears fell on the pages of her Bible. But when she stood again, Elsie's load of sorrow was gone, and as always, her heart was light with a sweet sense of peace and pardon.

She went back to her work with renewed diligence and faithfully completed all her assignments. When Miss Day returned from the fair, Elsie was able to recite her geography lesson without a single mistake. Her arithmetic problems were solved correctly, and the writing in her copybook was neat and careful.

But Miss Day, who had been in an ill-tempered mood all day, now seemed angry that Elsie did not give her another excuse for criticism. The governess handed the copybook back to the child and remarked sarcastically, "I see that you can do your duties well enough when you choose."

The injustice of Miss Day's words struck Elsie, and she wanted to protest that she had tried just as hard that morning. But she remembered her earlier, rash words and what they had cost her. Instead of defending herself, she meekly said, "I'm sorry I didn't do better this morning, though I really did try. I'm still more sorry for the disrespectful remark I made, and I ask your pardon."

"You ought to be sorry," replied Miss Day sharply, "and I hope you really are. You were very impertinent, and you deserved a more severe punishment than you received. Now go, and never let me hear anything like that from you again."

Elsie's eyes filled with tears again, but remembering how Jesus made no reply in the face of his accusers, she said nothing to Miss Day's hateful remarks. She simply put away her books and slate and left the schoolroom.

That evening, Rose was alone in her bedroom, thinking of her home and family so far away in the North, when she heard a gentle rapping at her door.

"Come in, darling," Rose greeted Elsie. "I'm so glad to see you."

Rose pointed to an ottoman, and Elsie, who had brought her little Bible, took her seat. "I may stay with you for half an hour; then Aunt Chloe is coming to put me to bed," she said.

Rose smiled. "It will be a pleasant half hour for us both."

Rose took her own Bible, and they read a chapter together, stopping now and then for Rose to give explanations. Then they knelt, and Rose offered a prayer for the teachings of the Spirit and for God's blessing on themselves and all their loved ones.

When they had risen, Rose folded the child in her arms and proclaimed gaily, "How I love you already, little Elsie. How glad I am that you love Jesus as I do and want to study His Word and pray."

"I'm not the only one," Elsie said with great seriousness. "Aunt Chloe loves Him too, very dearly."

"Then I must love her as well, for I have a special love for all who love my Savior."

With that, Rose sat down and put Elsie on her knee. Like old friends, they talked of the joys and challenges of Christian living and of the "race," as Paul the Apostle called it, that they were running and the "prize" they hoped to gain. They felt like pilgrims on the same path, and it was pleasant to walk awhile together.

A knock at the door interrupted their conversation, and a handsome, middle-aged black woman entered. She was extremely neat in her black dress, starched white apron, and turban-like headdress, and with a slight bow, she asked, "Is my little Elsie ready for bed now?"

"Yes, Aunt Chloe," said Elsie, running to her nursemaid's side, "but first I want to introduce you to Miss Allison."

Rose greeted her new guest warmly and took her hand. "How do you do, Aunt Chloe? I'm very glad to know you, since Elsie tells me you are a servant of the same Master I love and serve."

"Indeed I am, Miss Allison," Chloe said, grasping Rose's small hand in her two strong ones. "I love my precious Savior with all my heart."

"Then we are united through our faith in Him," Rose replied warmly. "For the Bible tells us that for all who love Him, there is neither Jew nor Greek, slave nor free, male nor female — we are all one in Christ."

Rose pressed Chloe's hands warmly, and between the two women — the one free and the other slave — the barriers of race and position melted away in the power of their shared faith.

Then reaching down, Chloe took Elsie's hand. "Good night now, Miss Allison. It's time I put this child to bed."

"Good night then, and please come again," Rose said. "And good night to you, little Elsie," she added, hugging the child again.

"What a blessed young lady," Chloe declared as she prepared Elsie for bedtime.

"Oh, Aunt Chloe, she's so good and kind, and she loves Jesus and loves to talk about Him," Elsie said happily.

"She reminds me of your mother, though she is not as beautiful. I think there never was a lady so beautiful as your mother."

Chloe brushed a tear from her eye as Elsie lifted the gold-framed miniature, which she wore day and night, and gave it a kiss. Then she slipped the chain inside her white nightdress. Chloe brushed back Elsie's hair and arranged the nightcap that protected Elsie's curls while she slept. "There now, darling," the nursemaid said, "you're ready for bed."

"Not quite yet, Aunt Chloe." Elsie knelt beside her bed and offered her evening prayer. Then she got her little Bible and began reading aloud from it as Chloe prepared herself for bed, removing her head scarf and replacing it with her own thick nightcap. Chloe, who was never willing to leave her charge for long, slept on a cot in one corner of the room.

When Elsie had finished her reading, she got into her bed, and Chloe tucked the covers securely around her.

"Please wake me early, Aunt Chloe, because I have a lesson to learn before breakfast."

"I will, darling," Chloe said as she snuffed out the light.

Rose Allison was an early riser and always spent an hour or two reading before the family gathered for breakfast at eight o'clock. She had asked Elsie to join her at seven-thirty, and punctually at that time, she heard the child's gentle tap on her door.

Elsie, looking as bright as the morning, carried her Bible and a bouquet of fresh flowers, which she presented to Rose with a graceful curtsy.

"I gathered these for you because I know you love flowers," Elsie said.

"Thank you, darling. They're lovely," Rose said, rewarding Elsie with a hug. "Now we can have our time together before breakfast."

The half hour passed so quickly that both were surprised when the breakfast bell rang.

This was the first of many happy mornings for Elsie. Rose spent the fall and winter with the Dinsmores, and most mornings and evenings she and Elsie read and prayed together. Rose was often amazed at the depth of the little girl's faith in God and knowledge of divine things, but Elsie had received the best of teaching. Chloe, though not formally educated, was an earnest Christian, and she had, from the beginning, endeavored to teach Elsie about Jesus. For most of that time, Chloe had been assisted in her mission by Mrs. Murray, the Scottish Presbyterian woman who had accompanied them to Roselands. It had only been a few months before that Mrs. Murray had suddenly been summoned home to Scotland. An intelligent and pious woman, Mrs. Murray had carefully instructed Elsie, and her and

Chloe's efforts to bring Elsie to a saving knowledge of Christ had been blessed.

Young as Elsie was, she already had a well-developed Christian character. Though not remarkably precocious in other respects, she seemed to have very clear and correct views on her duty to God and her neighbor. She was truthful in both word and deed, very strict in her observation of the Sabbath — unlike the rest of the Dinsmore family — diligent in her studies, respectful to her elders, polite and kind to everyone. She was gentle, sweet-tempered, patient, and forgiving to a remarkable degree.

It was natural that Rose Allison should become strongly attached to Elsie and that the child would return this affection. Elsie felt deeply the lack of sympathy and love in the Dinsmore household, and before Rose came, she had only Chloe, who deeply loved the child.

True, Adelaide often treated Elsie affectionately, but they were far apart in age and Adelaide had little time to spend with her young niece. Lora, who had a strong sense of justice, occasionally intervened and took Elsie's side when she was unfairly accused. But none of the Dinsmores seemed to really care for her, and Elsie was often lonely and sad. Her grandfather, Horace Dinsmore, Sr., treated her with complete neglect and usually spoke of her as "old Grayson's grandchild." Mrs. Dinsmore genuinely disliked her, as the child of the stepson for whom she had no fondness and as a future rival to her own daughters. The younger children, following the example of their parents, usually neglected Elsie and sometimes mistreated her. Miss Day, knowing that there was no danger her employers would object, vented on Elsie the spite she dared not show her other pupils. Again and again, Elsie was made to give up her playthings to Enna, and sometimes to

Arthur and Walter. This treatment often caused Elsie to struggle with her temper; had she possessed less of a meek and gentle spirit, her life might have been wretched indeed.

But in spite of it all, Elsie was the happiest person in the family, for she had peace in her heart and felt the joy which the Savior gives to His own. She constantly took her sorrows and troubles to Him, and the coldness and neglect of the others only drove her closer to her Heavenly Friend. While she had His love, she could not be unhappy, and her trials seemed to make her naturally amiable character even more lovely.

Still, she thought constantly of her absent father, and she longed intensely for his return. Day and night, she dreamed that he had come home, had taken her to his heart and called her his "own precious child" and his "precious little Elsie," just as her grandfather often spoke to Enna. But from month to month, year to year, her father's return was delayed, and her heart grew weary with its almost hopeless waiting.

There were pleasant times, however, and on the morning of her first session with Rose, Elsie got an unexpected surprise. When she and Rose entered the breakfast room, Adelaide called them aside.

"Elsie," her aunt began, "the fair isn't over yet, you know, and Miss Allison and I plan to ride there this afternoon. If you are a good girl in school this morning, you may go with us."

Elsie eyes glowed with happiness, and she clapped her hands in delight. "Oh, thank you, Aunt Adelaide. How kind you are!"

Miss Day, who overheard Adelaide's promise, frowned. Her immediate instinct was to reprove Elsie for her noisy outburst, but the governess was somewhat awed by Adelaide, and so she said nothing.

At that moment Mrs. Dinsmore entered, and Elsie instantly fell silent. She could rarely utter a word in her step-grandmother's presence without being scolded and told that "children should be seen and not heard" — even though Mrs. Dinsmore's own children were always allowed to talk as much as they pleased. But the entire family was silent that morning. Miss Day seemed cross, and Mrs. Dinsmore, complaining of a headache, was moody and taciturn. Mr. Dinsmore retreated behind his newspaper and said nothing. So Elsie was relieved when the meal concluded. She hurried to the schoolroom and began her lessons before the other children arrived.

She had been working on her arithmetic problems for about a half hour when the door opened and, to Elsie's dismay, Arthur entered. The boy did not begin his usual teasing and tormenting, however. Instead, he sat at his desk and rested his head on his hand in a dejected manner. Naturally Elsie wondered what was bothering her uncle, and she stole glances at him every now and then. Finally, she asked, "What's the matter, Arthur?"

"Nothing," he said gruffly and then turned his back on her.

Elsie said no more and returned to her studies. By the time the school day began, Elsie was so thoroughly prepared that Miss Day had no excuse for finding fault. Elsie's lessons were all completed on schedule, and she joined Adelaide and Rose for the promised ride to the fair.

They returned to Roselands about an hour before supper, and with time to herself, Elsie decided to finish a drawing that she had left in her school desk. While she was getting it and hunting for a pencil, she heard voices coming from the veranda. She recognized them as Lora's and Arthur's, but

she paid no attention to their conversation until her own name was mentioned.

"Elsie is the only person who can help you," Lora was saying.

"She has plenty of money, and you know that she is generous. But if I were you, I'd be ashamed to ask her, after the way you treated her yesterday."

"I wish I hadn't teased her," Arthur agreed, "but it's so much fun that I can't help myself."

"Well, I know that I wouldn't ask a favor of anybody whom I had treated so meanly," Lora said finally, and Elsie heard footsteps as the older girl walked away.

Elsie worked at her drawing, but her thoughts were of Arthur. What was it that he wanted? Was this an opportunity for her to return good for evil? She was hesitant to speak to him, but when she heard a deep sigh from the veranda, she left her drawing and went outside. Arthur was leaning against the railing; his head was bent and his eyes fixed on the ground. Without thinking, Elsie went to him, laid her hand on his shoulder, and asked if there was anything she could do to help.

"No — yes —" he answered haltingly. "I don't like to ask after — after —"

"Oh, never mind yesterday," Elsie said quickly. "I don't care about that now. I went to the fair today, and it was even better because I went with Aunt Adelaide and Miss Allison. So tell me what you want."

Encouraged, Arthur explained, "I saw a beautiful model of a ship when we were in the city yesterday, and I've set my heart on having it. It only costs five dollars, but my pocket money's all gone, and Papa won't give me a cent of allowance until next month. By that time, the ship will be gone because it's so beautiful someone is sure to buy it."

"Won't your mother buy it for you?" Elsie inquired.

"I asked, but she said she can't spare the money right now. It's so near the end of the month that we've all spent our allowances. Except Louise, but she says she won't lend money to a spendthrift like me."

Elsie took out her little purse and seemed ready to give it to Arthur. But she hesitated a moment, then returned it to her pocket. "Five dollars is a lot of money for a little girl like me," she said with a small smile. "I have to think about it, Arthur."

"I'm not asking you to *give* me money," Arthur contended. "I'll pay it back in two weeks."

Elsie only said, "Let me think about it until tomorrow morning," and she turned away from her disconsolate uncle. Arthur glanced at her retreating figure, and one angry word slipped from his lips: "Stingy."

But Elsie was still smiling as she ran down to the kitchen in search of Pompey, who was one of her special friends among the household servants. Finding him at last, she asked, "Pompey, are you going into the city tonight?"

"I am, Miss Elsie. I have some errands to do for Mrs. Dinsmore and the family, so I'll be leaving in about ten minutes. Is there something you want, eh?"

Elsie moved close and put her purse in Pompey's hand. Whispering, she told the old man about Arthur's wish and asked if he would take the money, and a half-dollar for his trouble, and purchase the coveted toy. And could he keep it secret from the others?

"I sure can do that," Pompey replied, a broad grin lighting his face. "I'll do this business just right for you."

When the supper bell rang, Elsie hurried to the dining room. Arthur sat across from her at the table, but when she

smiled at him, he only averted his eyes, and his face darkened with an angry scowl.

When Elsie retired to her room after her evening hour with Rose, Chloe pointed to an item on the mantle. It was the model ship.

"Arthur was right," Elsie exclaimed with delight. "It's a beauty! He's going to be so pleased. Aunt Chloe, could you take it to the schoolroom and put it on Arthur's desk? And be sure no one sees you?"

"I can try, darling," Chloe said, carefully taking the beautifully crafted little boat into her hand.

"Wait a minute," Elsie said with excitement. She took a notecard from her table and wrote on it: "A present to Arthur, from his niece, Elsie."

"There," she said, placing the card on the deck of the little model. "Now please, Aunt Chloe, check the hallway to be sure no one is there."

Chloe opened the bedroom door, and with exaggerated caution, she looked up and down the empty hall. "Coast is clear," she said. "All the children are in bed, I expect." Then taking a candle in her other hand, she disappeared out the door. A few minutes later, she returned, assuring Elsie that the task had been completed and "nobody's the wiser."

Elsie went to bed very happy that night, anticipating Arthur's pleasure.

On her way to breakfast the next morning, she was surprised by two hands seizing her around the waist. It was Arthur, who had just run in from the garden.

"Thank you, Elsie! You really are a good girl," he said, a huge smile filling his face. "The ship sails so well. I've been trying her on the pond. But it mustn't be a present. You have to let me pay you back."

"No, that would spoil my fun," Elsie insisted. "It's a gift, and you're welcome to it. Besides, my allowance is so large that I usually have more money than I can spend."

"I wish that were my problem," Arthur laughed. Then his smile vanished, and he said gently, "I'm sorry I teased you, Elsie. I won't do it again soon."

Arthur kept his word, and for many weeks, Elsie was able to complete her lessons with no annoyance from him. Miss Day, however, was often unreasonable and demanding. Scarcely a day went by that Elsie wasn't expected to give up her toys or inconvenience herself just to please Enna or Walter or someone else in the family. But still, the entire winter was unusually happy; Rose Allison's love and constant kindness, and her ability to draw out the thoughts and feelings in Elsie's heart, warmed the little girl's life like sunshine. Besides, Elsie had learned how to yield readily to others, and when she experienced some unjust or unkind treatment, she would go to her Bible. Her communings with her beloved Savior made everything right again, and she would emerge as serenely happy as if nothing had happened. Her attitude bewildered the family. Her grandfather would sometimes contemplate her behavior when she graciously gave up her wishes to Enna. Then he'd shake his head and say to himself, "That girl's no Dinsmore, or she'd stand up for her rights better than that. She can't be Horace's child, for it never was easy to impose on him. He was a boy of spirit, not like this child."

Even Adelaide had remarked to Rose that Elsie was a "strange" child. "I'm often surprised to see how sweetly she gives in to all of us," Adelaide observed. "Really, she has a lovely temperament. I envy her, for it was always hard for me to give up my own way or forgive those who teased me."

"I don't think it has been easy for Elsie either," Rose said. "But the Bible tells us that it is to a person's glory to overlook an offense. I think her sweet disposition is the fruit of a work of grace in her heart. It is 'the unfading beauty of a gentle and quiet spirit' which God alone can bestow."

"I wish I had that," Adelaide sighed.

"You only have to go to the right source, dear Adelaide," Rose replied kindly.

"And yet," Adelaide went on, "I must say that sometimes I think, as Papa says, that there is something mean-spirited and cowardly in always giving up to others."

"It would be cowardly and wrong to give up *principle*," Rose said, "but surely it is noble and generous to give up our own wishes to another, when no principle is involved."

"Of course, you're right," Adelaide mused. "And now that I think of it, although Elsie gives in on her wishes readily enough, I've never known her to sacrifice principle. On the contrary, she has made Mamma very angry several times by refusing to play with Enna on the Sabbath or to lie to Papa about Arthur's misdeeds. Elsie is certainly very different from the rest of us, and if it's godliness that makes her what she is, then I think godliness is a lovely thing."

Elsie spent her mornings in the schoolroom, and in the afternoons, she walked or went riding, sometimes with her young aunts and uncles and sometimes with Jim, one of the younger slaves and an excellent horseman, who was assigned to watch over her on her rides. There was always company at Roselands in the evening, but she usually preferred sitting with Aunt Chloe by the fire in her bedroom to

joining the guests in the parlor or playing with the other children in the sitting room or the playroom. When she had no lessons to learn, she often read aloud to Chloe, and the Bible was the book they both preferred. Sometimes Elsie would pull her little stool close by Chloe's side, put her head on the nursemaid's lap, and ask, "Please, Aunt Chloe, tell me about my mother."

Then, for the hundredth time or more, Chloe would recount the life and death of her "dear young mistress," as she called Elsie's mother. She would speak of the first Elsie's beauty, her goodness, and the sorrows she suffered during the last year of her short life. The story never lost its charms for little Elsie, and Chloe never tired of telling it. As Chloe spoke, Elsie would gaze at the miniature portrait of her mother, and when the story was finished, Elsie would say, "Now, tell me about Papa."

But about young Horace Dinsmore, Chloe had little information. She had known him only as a lively and handsome stranger whom she had seen occasionally during a few months and who had stolen the sunshine from her mistress, leaving her to die alone. Yet Chloe did not blame him when speaking to his child; her mistress had said that Horace did not desert her and their child of his own free choice. And even though Chloe could not believe him entirely blameless, she breathed no hint of her feeling to Elsie. Chloe was a sensible woman, and she knew that it would be hurtful to make her young charge think ill of her remaining parent.

Sometimes Elsie would ask if her Papa loved Jesus, and with a doubtful shake of her head, Chloe would say, "I don't know, darling, but I pray for him every day."

"So do I," Elsie would sigh. "How I wish he would come home."

And thus the winter glided away, and spring came, and with it the time approached when Rose Allison was to return to her family in Philadelphia. Her departure was scheduled for the second of April, and it was now the last day of March. For a number of weeks, Elsie had devoted all her spare time to knitting a purse; she wanted to give Rose something made with her own hands because she knew Rose would prize such a gift more than something more costly.

Elsie was in her room with Chloe. She had been knitting, and suddenly she held up the purse. "See!" she exclaimed. "It's all done except for putting on the tassel. Isn't it pretty, Aunt Chloe? Do you think Miss Allison will be pleased?"

It was, Chloe agreed, a very pretty purse, beautifully knit in crimson and gold, and she was sure Miss Allison would be delighted. They were admiring the purse when Enna opened the door and came in. Although Elsie tried to conceal the purse in her pocket, it was too late. Enna had seen it, and she ran to Elsie, crying, "Just give that to me, Elsie!"

When Elsie refused, explaining that it was a gift for Miss Allison, Enna raised her voice even more and demanded, "Give it to me now, or I'll go and tell Mamma!"

"I'll let you hold it for a few moments, if you promise not to soil it," Elsie said gently. "And if you like, I'll get more silk and beads and make you a purse just like it. But I can't give it to you because then I wouldn't have time to make another one for Miss Allison."

But Enna was adamant: "I want that now, and I want it to keep!" She tried to snatch the purse from Elsie's hand, but Elsie held it up out of the screaming child's reach. Finally Enna gave up and ran crying from the room.

39

Chloe locked the door, remarking that it was a pity they had forgotten to lock it earlier. "I'm afraid Miss Enna will get her mother to make you give it up," she said sadly.

Elsie went back to her work, but her eyes were full of tears and her hands trembled with agitation.

Chloe's fears were well founded, of course, and it was not very long before they heard hasty steps in the hallway and the rattling of the doorknob. When the door refused to open, Mrs. Dinsmore's booming voice commanded, "Open this door immediately!"

Chloe looked at Elsie. Tearfully, the little girl slipped the purse into her pocket again and lifted her heart in a quick prayer for patience and meekness, for she knew she would need both.

Chloe slowly unlocked the door, and Mrs. Dinsmore entered, with a sobbing Enna hanging onto her hand. The woman's face was flushed a bright red, and she spoke angrily to Elsie. "What is the meaning of this, you little good-for-nothing? Why are you always tormenting my poor Enna? Where is the pitiful thing that this fuss is all about? Let me see it at once!"

Elsie took the purse from her pocket. Her voice trembled as she said, "It's the purse I was making for Miss Allison. I'll make one just like it for Enna, but I cannot give her this one."

"You *can* not? You *will* not is what you mean. But I say you *shall*, and I am mistress in this house. Give it to Enna this instant. I will not have her crying her eyes out just to humor you in your whims. There are plenty of more handsome purses in the city, and if you are too mean to give this one to Enna, then I will buy you another one tomorrow."

"But that wouldn't be my work," Elsie protested, still holding the purse to herself. "This is."

"Nonsense! What difference will it make to Rose anyway?" With those words, Mrs. Dinsmore grabbed the purse from Elsie and gave it to Enna. "There, my little one," she said in a cooing tone to her blubbering child. "It's yours now. Elsie is a naughty, mean, stingy girl, but she won't plague you when your mother is about."

Enna threw a look of spiteful triumph at Elsie and then ran from the room with her prize. Her mother followed, as Elsie collapsed on Chloe's lap and cried bitterly. Chloe had to call on all her faith in God to hold down the anger and indignation she felt. She let Elsie sob for a few minutes, soothing her only with silent caresses, and allowed her own fury to subside. Then she said, "Never mind, child. You just go into the city tomorrow and buy the prettiest purse you can find for Miss Allison."

But Elsie shook her head. "I wanted it to be my own work," she sobbed, "and now there's no time."

Chloe had a sudden thought. "I'll tell you what, pet. Remember the purse you were knitting for your father? The one Mrs. Dinsmore wouldn't send for you? Well, you can get that finished for Miss Allison, then knit another for your Papa before he comes home."

Elsie raised eyes full of relief, though they clouded almost at once. "But I don't have any beads to finish it, and Miss Rose leaves the day after tomorrow."

Chloe, however, would not be discouraged. "Pompey is going into the city this very afternoon," she said, "so we'll ask him to buy the beads. Then you can finish the purse by tomorrow evening and give it to Miss Allison before she leaves. It's going to be just fine."

"You're right, Aunt Chloe," Elsie said excitedly. "Thank you for thinking of it."

She went to her bureau and unlocked a drawer from which she carefully withdrew a purse of gold and blue beads — quite as handsome as the one taken from her — and she rolled it in a piece of tissue paper. She handed the small bundle to Chloe, who hurried away in search of Pompey. But Pompey informed her that with all his other errands, he wouldn't have time to attend to Elsie's needs. Chloe, who knew that Pompey was very fond of the child, believed him and didn't push the request. What could she do?

"I'll go myself, " she suddenly decided. "I'll ride with you, Pompey, and get the beads and silk myself."

She checked first that Elsie would not need her that afternoon, for Chloe was Elsie's servant only, with responsibilities for no one else in the family. Then she joined Pompey for the trip to the city. But it was late before they returned, and Elsie spent the evening alone in her room. She didn't even have her hour with Rose, who remained with the guests in the parlor that night.

At 'st, Chloe was back, with all the things Elsie needed. She wanted to begin her work immediately, but before she could start, a servant came to the door with a note. It was from Rose Allison.

"Dear Elsie," the note began. "I am very sorry that we cannot have our reading together this evening, but be sure to come early in the morning. It will be our last opportunity, for I have another disappointment for you. I had not expected to leave until the day after tomorrow, but I've just learned that the ship will sail a day sooner, and therefore I am obliged to begin my journey tomorrow. Your friend, Rose."

Elsie dropped the note on the floor and burst into tears. "Oh, no! Dear Miss Allison is going home tomorrow," she sobbed. But she soon stopped her crying, dried her tears, and gathered the items Chloe had brought from the city.

"I must finish the work tonight," she said firmly, and she set about her task. And though she did not sleep many hours that night, Elsie arrived at Rose's door at precisely seven-thirty the next morning.

Rose clasped the child in her arms as Elsie sobbed, "Dear, dear, Miss Rose, what shall I do without you?"

"You have a better Friend, Elsie, one who said 'I will never leave you nor forsake you,'" Rose whispered.

"And He is your friend, too," Elsie said as she wiped her tears. "Don't you think He will bring us together again some day?"

"I hope so indeed. And we must keep very close to Him, Elsie. We must commune with Him, and study His Word, and try always to do His will. If we have the assurance that our dear Friend is with us — that we have His presence and His love — we shall be supremely happy even though separated from our earthly friends. I know you have peculiar trials, little one, and you often feel the lack of sympathy and love here. But you will always find them in Jesus."

With this reassurance, Elsie and Rose shared their last morning of reading and prayer. Rose read the fourteenth chapter of John, a part of the Savior's touching farewell to His disciples. Then they knelt to pray, although Elsie's heart was so full that she could only listen.

"We will hope to meet again before very long," Rose said when her prayer was ended. "Who knows? Your father may come home and bring you to see me someday. He likes to travel, so it seems a good possibility."

Smiling now, Elsie said, "That would be wonderful!" Then she added, with a deep sigh, "But sometimes it seems that my Papa will never come home."

Cheerfully, Rose said, "Well, we can hope. And even though we must be separated for a time, we can still meet in spirit at the mercy-seat. Let's agree to do it every morning at this hour, shall we?"

The idea was a happy one for Elsie, and she eagerly assented.

"And I will write to you, dear," Rose continued. "I will write while I am traveling, if I can, so you will receive my letter a week from now. Then you must write to me. Will you?"

"If you won't care about my mistakes, Miss Rose," Elsie replied a little self-consciously. "I can't ask Miss Day to correct my letter because I don't want her to read it. But I will be so glad to get yours. I've never had a letter in my whole life."

"I won't care at all about mistakes," Rose assured, "and no one will see your letters except me. I don't want Miss Day reading them either."

Rose reached to hug Elsie once more, and the girl's hand went into her pocket, bringing out the finished gold and blue purse. "It's all my own work because I thought you would value it more," Elsie said shyly.

"And indeed I shall!" Rose said. "It's a beautiful purse in itself, but I will value it ten times more because it is your gift and the work of your hands." She hugged her little friend close, and Elsie, so unused to praise for her accomplishments, felt a kind of warmth she had hardly ever known.

They had only a few more minutes together, for immediately after breakfast, Rose's carriage arrived. The family,

who had all come to care for their visitor and would miss her presence in their house, gathered at the door to bid her farewell. One by one, they said their good-byes, and Elsie was the last. Rose kissed the child tenderly, and choking back her tears, she said, "God bless and keep you, my poor little darling, my dear little Elsie."

Elsie simply could not speak, and when the carriage had rolled out of sight, she ran to her room, locked the door, and cried out her grief. She had learned to love Rose completely and to depend on her new friend without reservation. Parting, with no certainty of ever meeting again, was one of the hardest trials the child had ever endured.

CHAPTER

3

An Unexpected Homecoming

"Hope deferred makes the heart sick, but a longing fulfilled is a tree of life."

PROVERBS 13:12

An Unexpected Homecoming

It had been a week since Rose Allison's departure — a lonely week for Elsie — and at the breakfast table, Adelaide voiced the little girl's own thoughts. "I think we ought to hear from Rose soon," Adelaide said. "She promised to write during her journey."

Almost in answer to her words, Pompey entered the room, carrying the mail bag which he brought from the city every morning. He handed the bag to Mr. Dinsmore as Mrs. Dinsmore remarked, with some irritation, "You're late this morning, Pompey."

"Yes, ma'am," replied the old servant, smiling sweetly. "The horses were very lazy today. I expect they have spring fever."

"Do hurry, Papa," Adelaide said impatiently, "and see if there isn't something from Rose."

"Have patience, young lady," her father replied as he opened the bag and very deliberately adjusted his spectacles before sorting through the family's letters. "Yes, there is a letter here for you, and one for Elsie, too."

He tossed the letters across the table, and Elsie, being excused, eagerly grabbed hers and ran up to her room. It was like a feast for her — the first letter she had ever received — and from such a dear friend. For the moment at least, it gave her almost as much pleasure as Rose's presence would have.

Elsie had just finished reading the letter through and was beginning to read it again when she heard Adelaide calling. The next moment, her aunt entered the room.

"I suppose you've read your letter," Adelaide said, and a strange smile played on her mouth, "but now I have another piece of news for you. Can you guess it?"

Elsie's Endless Wait

"Is Miss Rose coming back?" Elsie ventured hopefully.

"What a silly guess," Adelaide said. "No, little Elsie, it's even more exciting. My brother — your Papa Horace — has actually sailed for America and is coming directly home."

Elsie jumped up, and her heart beat wildly. "Is it really true, Aunt Adelaide?" she asked. "Is he really coming? Will he be here soon?"

"He has really started at last," Adelaide assured, "but I don't know how soon he will be here." As she turned to leave, she added, "I've told you all that I know for the moment."

Elsie clapped her hands together and dropped down onto the sofa. The letter from Rose, so highly prized a few moments before, drifted unnoticed to the floor. The child's thoughts were now far away, imagining the father she didn't know as he crossed the ocean for home. She tried to picture how he would look, how he would speak, and how he would feel about her.

"Oh, will he love me?" she asked herself aloud. "Will he let me love him? Will he take me in his arms and call me his own darling child?"

But there was no one to answer her anxious questions. She would just have to wait and let the slow wheel of time turn until her father's longed-for, and somehow frightful, arrival.

In the schoolroom, Elsie recited her lessons indifferently until Miss Day sternly remarked that receiving letters did not seem to agree with her pupil. Elsie must do better, Miss Day said, if she wished to please her Papa when he came. For once, Miss Day's observation struck just the right chord; Elsie was extremely anxious to please her father and

to gain his affection and approval. She turned her whole attention to her studies with such determination that Miss Day could find no more cause for complaint.

But what, indeed, did the father expect of his daughter? Horace Dinsmore, Jr., was, like his father, an upright and moral man who paid outward respect to the forms of religion but cared nothing for the vital power of godliness. Horace trusted his own morality entirely, and he regarded most Christians as hypocrites and deceivers. He had been told of his little Elsie's Christian devotion, and though he didn't acknowledge it even to himself, this information had prejudiced him against his child.

Also, like all the Dinsmores, he had a great deal of family pride. Although his wife's father, Mr. Grayson, had been a man of sterling worth — intelligent, honest, pious, and very wealthy at his death — he had begun life as a poor boy and made his fortune in business. For this reason, all the Dinsmores spoke of Horace's marriage to his beautiful heiress as a step down. Even Horace himself had come to regard his marriage as a boyish folly of which he was now ashamed. So often in his letters had Mr. Dinsmore referred to Elsie as "old Grayson's grandchild" that Horace had come to think of her as a kind of disgrace, especially because she was always described to him as disagreeable and troublesome.

Horace had loved his young wife with genuine passion and mourned her death bitterly. But distance and the passage of so much time had dimmed his memory of her, and he seldom thought of her now except in connection with the

child, the child for whom, in his secret heart, he harbored a feeling of dislike.

At Roselands, scarcely anything was spoken or thought about outside of Horace's anticipated return, and for Elsie especially, the time crawled by. At last a letter came from Horace saying that he would arrive the next day.

"Oh, Aunt Chloe," said Elsie, jumping up and down and clapping her hands at the news. "Just think! Papa will be here tomorrow morning."

Then her wild delight turned sober, and concern clouded her face as the torturing question came again into her mind: *Will he love me?* She stood still now, as Chloe changed her from a riding outfit to a dress and smoothed her curls. Looking into the somber little face, Chloe couldn't resist hugging her little charge and pressing a gentle kiss on her brow.

It was at this moment that an unusual sense of activity seemed to fill the house. Elsie jumped, and the color rushed to her face as she listened intently. She heard the sound of running feet in the hall, and suddenly her door was flung open. "He's here!" Walter shouted as he grabbed her hand and pulled her from the room and down the stairs. But as they approached the parlor door, Elsie begged Walter to stop. She leaned against the wall, and her heart beat so fast she could scarcely breathe. This was the moment she had prayed for; yet she was unprepared and filled with fears she could not comprehend.

"Are you sick?" Walter asked, but not waiting for a reply, he pushed the door open and dragged her inside. Elsie was

so overwrought that she almost fainted. The room seemed to spin, and for an instant, she hardly knew where she was.

Then a strange voice asked, "And who is this?" She looked up and saw a man — very handsome and youthful looking, in spite of his heavy, dark beard and mustache.

"Is this great girl *my* child?" Horace asked. "Why it's enough to make a man feel old." Then he took her hand, stooped, and kissed her coldly on the lips.

Elsie was shaking violently, and the power of her feelings made her incapable of speech. Her hand, still in his, was cold and clammy.

Horace searched her face, then dropped her hand. "I'm not an ogre," he said in a voice that betrayed his annoyance. "You need not be afraid of me. Alright, you may go. I won't keep you in terror any longer."

Dismissed, Elsie could only run back to her room where she fell onto the bed and wept as she never had before. For as long as she could remember, she had longed for this hour, yet the disappointment was so deep that it seemed her heart would break. Not even Chloe — who was in the kitchen, rejoicing in the assumption that her young charge was supremely happy at this moment — was there to offer comfort. Alone, Elsie wept as if she might weep her life away.

"Oh, Papa! Papa! You don't love me! Oh, Mamma, I wish I could be with you. There's no one here to love me, and I'm so lonely!"

This was how Chloe found her an hour later, still sobbing out her broken cries of anguish. Chloe understood at once how her child was suffering. She raised Elsie in her arms and cradled her feverish head, smoothing back the tear-sodden curls and bathing the child's swollen eyes and throbbing temples.

"My poor baby," she soothed. "You know your Aunt Chloe loves you better than life. And did you forget your Almighty Friend who loves you and says 'I will never leave you nor forsake you'? He sticks to us 'closer than a brother,' my precious child. Jesus' love is better than any other love, and I know you have His love."

"Then ask Him to take me to Himself, and to Mamma. I'm so lonely, and I want to die!"

"Hush, darling, hush now. I could never ask that. It would break my heart. You mean the world to me, and you know we must all wait for the Lord's time."

"Then ask Him to help me be patient," Elsie begged. "And ask Him to make my father love me."

"I will, darling, I will," Chloe said through her own tears. "And don't you be discouraged right away. I'm sure your Papa will love you once he comes to know you."

That evening, when the family gathered for supper, there was an empty chair at the table, and Adelaide sent one of the servants to find Elsie. When the woman returned, it was with the news that Elsie had a bad headache and didn't want to eat. Horace overheard the message, and he asked his sister, "Is she subject to such attacks? I hope she isn't a sickly child."

"Not really," Adelaide replied dryly. She had observed Horace's meeting with his child, and she felt really sorry for Elsie's evident disappointment. "I imagine that excessive crying has brought this on."

Horace flushed deeply, and in a caustic tone that betrayed his displeasure, he said, "So the return of a parent is a cause for grief, is it? I didn't expect my presence to be so distressing for my only child. I had no idea she disliked me so."

"She doesn't," Adelaide said, her own temper rising. "She has been looking forward to your return for as long as I've known her."

"That's hard to believe," Horace retorted, "given her conduct toward me today."

Adelaide could see that Horace was determined to misconstrue Elsie's behavior. She was afraid that any defense of the child would only increase his sour mood, so she said no more.

Upstairs in her bedroom, Elsie finally fell asleep, but not before she had turned in her sadness to Him who said, "I have loved you with an everlasting love." At least she had the sweet assurance of His love and favor.

The next morning Elsie came to breakfast in a state of hope and fear; she wanted, yet dreaded, meeting her father. But when she entered the dining room, he was not there.

"Your Papa isn't coming down this morning," Adelaide told her kindly. "He is very tired from his long journey. I'm sorry, but you may not see him at all today, for we expect a good deal of company this afternoon and tonight."

Disappointed once again, Elsie found it impossible to concentrate on her lessons. Every time the door opened, she jumped nervously and looked up, hoping it was her father. But Horace did not come to her, and that evening, the children were sent to dine in the playroom because there were so many guests for supper. Just as Adelaide had predicted, Elsie didn't see her father at all that day.

The next morning, however, the children were to breakfast with the adults because all the guests, except one gentleman,

had departed. Elsie went early into the breakfast room, and to her surprise, she found her father alone, reading the morning newspaper.

He looked up, and she said in a trembling voice, "Good morning, Papa." The greeting made Horace start, for he had never before been addressed as "Papa," and it sounded strange to his ears. He regarded his child with curiosity and almost reached out to her. But instead of extending his hand, he simply said, "Good morning, Elsie," and returned to his paper.

Elsie remained in the middle of the room; she didn't dare to approach him, however much she wanted to. While she stood there, not knowing what to do, the door swung open, and Enna, looking rosy and happy, ran in and rushed to her brother. She climbed on his knee, put her chubby arms around his neck, and pleaded for a kiss.

"You shall have it, little pet," Horace laughed. Tossing down his paper, he hugged Enna warmly. "*You* are not afraid of me, are you?" he asked playfully, and added pointedly, "or sorry that I have come home?"

"No, indeed," Enna said.

Horace glanced at Elsie to see her reaction. Her eyes had filled with tears, and she could not stop herself thinking that Enna had taken her place and was receiving the love that should be hers. Horace read her reaction correctly, although he misunderstood its source. "She's jealous," he thought. "I cannot tolerate jealous people." He gave her a look that clearly displayed his displeasure, and Elsie, cut to the quick, had to leave the room to hide her tears.

"I am envious," she thought. "I'm jealous of Enna. Oh, how awful of me!" Silently she prayed, "Dear Savior, help me! Take away these terrible feelings."

An Unexpected Homecoming

Despite her youth, Elsie was beginning to learn how to control her own emotions, and in a few moments, she had recovered her composure so that she could return to the breakfast room and take her place at the table. Her sweet face was sad indeed and showed the traces of tears, but it was also calm and peaceful.

Her father took no notice of her, and she didn't trust herself to look at him. The servants filled her plate, and she ate in silence. To her great relief, the others were too busy talking and eating to pay attention to her, and she failed to see how often the visitor who was seated nearly opposite her fixed his eyes on her pale face.

When she had left the room, the visitor asked, "Is that one of your sisters, Horace?"

"No," said Horace, flushing slightly. "She is my daughter."

"Ah! I'd almost forgotten that you have a child," the man said. "Well, you have no reason to be ashamed of her. She is perfectly lovely. Sweetest little face I ever saw."

Anxious to change the subject, Horace suggested to his friend that they call for their horses and take a ride around the property. The subject of Elsie was dropped, and the two men left together.

Several hours later, Elsie was practicing at the piano in the music room when she felt suddenly that she was not alone. Turning around, she recognized her father's friend as Edward Travilla, the owner of a neighboring plantation.

"Excuse me for interrupting," he said and bowed politely. "I heard the sound of the piano. I am very fond of music, so I ventured in."

Elsie was timid with outsiders, but she was also very polite, so she welcomed the guest. "Won't you take a seat,

sir? I'm afraid my music won't give you any pleasure. I'm only learning and cannot play very well yet."

Edward thanked her and took a seat near her side. "Will you do me a favor and repeat the song I heard you singing a few minutes ago?"

Though her cheeks were burning and her voice trembled at first, Elsie complied, and as she proceeded, her voice grew strong and steady. She had quite a nice voice for a girl her age, and she also had musical talent, which had been well cultivated by good teachers and diligent practice. Her music was simple, but her performance was very good.

Edward thanked her heartily and complimented both her playing and her singing. Then he asked for another song and another, and they chatted genially until Elsie lost all sense of embarrassment,

"I think your name is Elsie, isn't it?" Edward asked.

"Yes, sir. Elsie Dinsmore."

"And you are the daughter of my friend Horace Dinsmore?"

"Yes, sir."

"Your father has been gone for a long time, so I suppose you must have forgotten him."

"Oh, no, sir. I couldn't have forgotten him because I'd never seen him."

"Indeed," Edward remarked in surprise. "Then, since he is a stranger to you, I suppose you can't have much affection for him."

Elsie looked into his face, her hazel eyes very round, and said with astonishment, "Not love Papa? My own Papa who has no other child but me? Oh, Mr. Travilla, how could you think that?"

"I see I was mistaken," he said with a smile. "I see you care very much for your Papa. But do you think he loves you?"

To the gentleman's great dismay, Elsie dropped her face into her hands and burst into a torrent of tears. Trying to comfort her as best he could, Edward patted her quaking shoulder and said, "My poor child, forgive me. I am very, very sorry for my silly question. But trust me, dear girl, that whether your father loves you now or not, I know he will quite soon."

When Elsie had dried her tears and closed the piano, Edward invited her to take a little walk with him in the garden. He felt very sorry for the pain his thoughtless remark had inflicted, and the little girl interested him, so he did his best to entertain her as they walked. He talked to her about the plants and flowers. He told her about the foreign lands he had visited, and he related stories of his travels, deliberately choosing incidents in which her father had also played a part.

He discovered that Elsie was far from a dull companion. With a natural love of reading and ready access to her grandfather's well-stocked library, Elsie had read more books, and with more thought, than most children her age. The intelligence of her questions and conversation surprised and pleased Edward Travilla.

When the dinner bell rang, he escorted Elsie to the table and seated her at his side. Never was any great lady more carefully waited on than was Elsie at this meal. There were several more gentleman guests present who attended to the older women, so Edward felt at liberty to devote his attention to Elsie, talking to her — and making her talk.

Now and then, Elsie stole a glance at Mrs. Dinsmore, and to her great relief, the woman was too occupied to notice

her. Once Elsie glanced at her father, and when their eyes met, his held an expression that was both curious and amused — a look she could not interpret. But since she saw no displeasure there, her heart grew light and her face glowed with happiness.

Later, in the drawing room, as Horace and his old friend talked alone, Edward said, "Really, Horace, your daughter is remarkably intelligent, as well as remarkably pretty. And I've discovered that she has a good deal of musical talent."

"Has she?" Horace replied. "Perhaps it's a pity she doesn't belong to you, my friend, instead of me, for you seem to appreciate her so much more highly."

"I wish she did," Edward said. "But seriously, Horace, you ought to love that child. She certainly loves you devotedly."

Surprised by his friend's assessment, Horace asked, "How do you know?"

"It was clear from what I saw and heard this morning. Horace, she would value a kind word from you more than the richest jewel."

"I doubt that," Horace said, but there was a hint of a question in his words. He turned to the window, and suddenly, without explanation to his friend, he left the room, for he had seen Elsie come out onto the portico. She was dressed in her riding clothes, and Jim, who usually accompanied her when she rode by herself, was bringing up her horse.

Horace approached his daughter and asked, "Are you going for a ride, Elsie?"

"Yes, Papa," she said and looked shyly into his face.

Horace leaned down and lifted her into his arms. Then he placed her in the saddle, saying to the boy, "Now, Jim, you must take good care of my little girl."

This time, the tears that came to Elsie's eyes were for joy. "He called me *his* little girl," she murmured to herself as she rode away, "and he told Jim to take good care of me. I'm sure he will love me soon, just as Mr. Travilla said he would."

From the portico, Horace watched his daughter as she rode down the long avenue that led from the house. He didn't notice Edward Travilla, who had come out to join him.

"How well she sits her horse," Edward said.

"Yes, she does," Horace replied in an absent way. He was thinking of a time some eight or nine years before when he had assisted another Elsie to mount her horse and had ridden for hours at her side. For the rest of that afternoon, memories came flooding into his mind, and in his heart, a feeling of tenderness began to grow for the child of the wife who had been so dear to him. When he saw little Elsie returning up the driveway, he hurried outside again, lifted her from the horse, and asked if she had enjoyed her ride.

"Oh, yes, Papa. It was very pleasant."

He looked into her beaming face, and without thinking, he kissed his child warmly. "I think I will ride with you one of these days," he said. "Would you like that?"

"Oh, very much, Papa. So very much."

Horace smiled at his daughter's earnestness and watched her as she raced away to her room to change her clothes and tell Chloe of her happiness.

Alas, the moment was like a transient gleam of sunshine that lighted her path briefly, then disappeared behind gathering clouds.

Elsie's Endless Wait

More company came to Roselands, and the drawing room was filled with guests that evening. Though Elsie was there, her father was too busy with his guests to give her even a glance. She sat alone and unnoticed in a corner and watched her father's every move. Her ears strained to catch his words. Then Edward Travilla, who had been talking with a group on the opposite side of the room, disengaged himself and came toward Elsie. Taking her hand, he led her to the center table where a pleasant-looking, elderly lady was examining some engravings that Horace had brought home from Europe.

"Mother," said Edward, "this is my friend Elsie."

"I am so glad to see you, my dear," the lady said, giving Elsie a kiss.

Edward set a chair for Elsie close to his mother, and he sat on the child's other side. He began to explain the engravings, and since he attached a clever anecdote to each, Elsie was thoroughly entertained and quite forgot to look for her father.

Suddenly, Edward laid down the engraving he was describing and said, "Miss Elsie, I want my mother to hear you play and sing. Will you do me the favor of repeating the song I admired so much this morning?"

Elsie blushed brightly and exclaimed, "I couldn't play or sing for so many people, Mr. Travilla. Please excuse me."

But from behind her, Horace's voice commanded, "Go immediately, and do as the gentleman requests."

His voice was stern, and Elsie saw that his face was even more so. Trembling, she rose to obey, but Edward, who could see her distress, said kindly, "Never mind, Miss Elsie. I withdraw my request."

"But I do not withdraw my command," her father said. "Go at once, Elsie, and do as I say."

She went, and Edward, silently scolding himself for causing her trouble, placed her sheet of music on the piano and whispered encouragingly in her ear, "Have confidence in yourself, Miss Elsie. That is all that is necessary for your success."

But Elsie was shattered by her father's attitude, and she could not control the tears that welled in her eyes. She could barely see the notes and words, and she blundered badly as she attempted to play the prelude. Her mistakes only increased her misery and embarrassment.

"Never mind the prelude," Edward said in an effort to help. "You can just begin the song."

But it was no use. Before she could get through the first verse, she broke into tears. Her father, looking mortified, came up behind her and spoke in low, hard tones, "Elsie, I am ashamed of you. Go to your room and to bed immediately."

Again she obeyed, and again, she cried herself to sleep.

The next morning, Elsie learned that Edward Travilla and his mother had returned to their home. Elsie was very sorry that she hadn't said good-bye to her new friends, and for the next few days, her sorrow increased, for her father's cold manner had returned. He scarcely ever spoke to her, and to make matters worse, her young aunts and uncles ridiculed her for the failed attempt to play at the party.

Even Miss Day, who seemed unusually cross, taunted her. Elsie tried to pay attention to her lessons, but she was so troubled and depressed that she failed repeatedly and was in constant disgrace with Miss Day, who threatened to go to her father. When Miss Day saw how this threat terrified Elsie, the governess used it all the more.

But what chiefly occupied Elsie's thoughts was how to gain her father's love. She tried every way she could to win

his affection. She cheerfully obeyed his every order and tried to anticipate and fulfill his wishes. But he seldom seemed to notice her except for commands and rebukes, while he lavished attention on his sister Enna. Elsie could only watch them in silence until her feelings overwhelmed her and she rushed away to cry in secret and to pray for her father's love. She never complained, not even to Chloe, but the anxious nursemaid clearly saw that her beloved child was very unhappy.

"Maybe you should be more like Enna," Chloe suggested. "Be merry and run and jump on your Papa's knee. I think he'll like you better for it."

But the very thought terrified Elsie. "I can't do that," she said mournfully. "I don't dare."

So as Elsie grew increasingly pale and melancholy, Chloe's heart ached, and she, too, shed many secret tears.

CHAPTER 4

New Rules

"Children, obey your parents in everything, for this pleases the Lord."

COLOSSIANS 3:20

So things went for about a week, until the morning when Elsie entered the breakfast room to be greeted by her father with an unusually pleasant "Good morning, Elsie." Then he took her hand and led her to the seat beside his at the table. Elsie, so used to being ignored, nearly glowed with pleasure.

There were several guests present, and Elsie waited patiently while they and the older members of the family were served. When her turn came, her grandfather asked, "Have some bacon, Elsie?"

But before she could answer, her father said, "None for Elsie. Once a day is often enough for a child to eat meat. She may have it for dinner at mid-day, but never at breakfast or supper."

Old Mr. Dinsmore laughed, "Really, Horace, where did you get such a notion? I always allowed you to eat whatever you pleased, and I never saw it hurt you. But, of course, you must manage your child in your own way."

When hot cakes were passed, Horace again said none for Elsie. Instead he placed a slice of bread on her plate and explained, "I don't approve of hot cakes and rolls and muffins for children, so you must eat only cold bread."

And as old Pompey was about to set a cup of coffee down for Elsie, Horace intervened again. "Take the coffee away, please," Horace said, "and bring Elsie a tumbler of milk. Or would you prefer water, Elsie?"

"Milk, please, Papa," the little girl replied with a small sigh. She was very fond of coffee, and it was not easy to give up.

Horace spooned a serving of stewed fruit onto her plate, and Pompey returned with her milk. "There," her father said. "You have your breakfast. In England, children are not allowed to eat butter until they are ten or twelve years old, and I think it's an excellent plan to make them grow rosy and healthy. I have neglected my little girl for too long," he added, smiling and laying his hand on her head for a moment. "But I intend to take good care of you now."

Whatever the cause for this change in him, his words and his manner were more than enough to reconcile Elsie to her meager meal, and she ate with relish. But the meager fare became a constant, and Elsie often looked longingly at the hot buttered rolls and cups of coffee enjoyed by the others. She tried to content herself with the assurance that her Papa was doing what was best for her and to remind herself that Jesus would be pleased with her obedience, but it was not so easy to understand these new rules.

One morning as he read in the drawing room, Horace overheard Arthur teasing Elsie as usual. "Isn't it great to have your Papa home?" the boy was saying snippily. "And how pleasant for you to live on bread and water, eh!"

"I don't live on bread and water," Elsie replied indignantly.

"Papa allows me as much milk and cream and fruit as I want. I can have eggs and cheese and honey and anything else except meat and hot cakes and butter and coffee. And I wouldn't trade any of those things for a father who loves me. Besides, Papa says I can have all the meat I want for dinner."

Arthur became even more scornful. "That's nothing," he mocked. "And I wouldn't give much for all the love *you* get from him."

New Rules

The last Horace heard was what sounded like a sob, and he went to the window in time to catch a glimpse of Elsie running down the garden path.

Horace found Arthur just outside, leaning lazily against one of the pillars on the portico, "What do you mean, sir, teasing Elsie in that manner?" Horace demanded.

"I only wanted to have a little fun," Arthur replied sullenly.

"Well, I don't approve of that kind of fun, and you will leave the child alone in the future," Horace commanded.

Returning to the drawing room, Horace picked up his newspaper again, but it no longer held his interest. He kept hearing that little sob and seeing his child running from his brother's hateful taunts. When the ringing of the school bell broke into his thoughts, he tossed his paper down, took a card from his pocket, jotted a few words on it, and called a servant to take the note to Miss Day.

When the note was delivered, Miss Day looked at it and said to Elsie, "Your father wants you. You may go."

With some trepidation, Elsie left the schoolroom and hurried to find her father. Fanny, one of the housekeeping servants, directed her to the drawing room.

When Elsie entered, Horace smiled and held out his hand to her. "Come here, Daughter," he said, and her little heart thrilled, for he had never called her "Daughter" before. She stood at his side, and he took her hand in one of his, placed his other hand gently on her head, and looked deeply into her eyes.

"You've been crying" he said in a gently reproving tone. "I'm afraid you do a good deal more crying than is good for you. It is a very babyish habit, and you must try to break yourself of it."

She flushed, and in spite of herself, her eyes filled.

But Horace stroked her hair softly and said, "Don't begin it again. I have good news for you. I plan to drive over to Ion today, to see Mr. Travilla and his mother, and I would like you to go with me."

"Oh, thank you, Papa," she said eagerly.

"There are no little folks there, but I can see you want to go. Now run along and ask Aunt Chloe to get you ready, and tell her to dress you nicely. The carriage will be here for us in half an hour."

Elsie bounded away, and at the specified time, she came back, looking so pretty that her father gazed at her in proud delight and gave her a kiss as he lifted her into the carriage.

"Have you ever been to Ion?" he asked as the coachman guided the horses on their journey,

"No, sir, but I've heard Aunt Adelaide say it's a very lovely place."

"So it is, though not as pretty as Roselands," Horace said. "Edward Travilla and I have been friends since our boyhood, and I spent many happy days at Ion — long before I ever thought of you."

He smiled and patted her cheek.

"Tell me about those times, please, Papa," Elsie asked. "It seems so strange that you were ever a little boy, and I was nowhere."

Horace laughed and then said thoughtfully, "It seems just a short time ago, to me, that I was no older than you are now."

But instead of telling her more, Horace lapsed into silence. They drove on without speaking for some time, until Elsie spotted a squirrel darting up a tree, and she exclaimed, "Did you see that squirrel? Look, Papa, he's perched on that branch."

The coach moved on, and the squirrel was out of sight, but Elsie's outburst, far from annoying her father, reminded him of a day he had once spent hunting squirrels in those very woods. He gave Elsie a very animated account, including the moment when one of his companions accidentally fired his hunting rifle, and the bullet missed Horace by a hair's breadth.

"I felt like fainting when I realized how near I'd come to death," he concluded.

"Oh, Papa, how good God was to save you. If you'd been killed, I could never have had you for my father."

"Perhaps you would have had a better one, Elsie," he said.

Elsie was about to protest, but just then the carriage turned into a broad, tree-lined drive, and Horace cheerfully announced, "There it is, Elsie dear. There is Ion."

In another few minutes, they were alighting from the carriage, and Edward Travilla was greeting them. "Why, Horace, you've brought my little friend Elsie. This is really good of you," he said with genuine delight. The men shook hands enthusiastically, and Edward planted a little kiss on Elsie's cheek. Then he led them inside. "My mother will be so happy to see you both," he said, "and she seems to have taken a special fancy to Miss Elsie."

Mrs. Travilla's greeting was no less cordial, though somewhat less boisterous, than her son's, and she made Elsie feel at home immediately. When the men had left to tour the plantation, the woman and the girl spent an enjoyable morning together in Mrs. Travilla's room. They chatted, and Elsie helped Mrs. Travilla with some garments she was making for the field hands. Elsie soon learned that Mrs. Travilla was a devoted Christian — a tie that drew

them closer. Mrs. Travilla was also a discerning woman; she had known Horace nearly all his life, and she already had some notion of the difficulties of Elsie's situation. Without alluding to anything specific, she nevertheless gave the little girl some excellent advice, for which Elsie was truly grateful.

Several hours had passed when Edward returned. "Come, Elsie. I want you to see my garden and hothouse. Will you come, Mother? We have just enough time before dinner."

"No, Edward, I have some things to attend to. So you do the honors," Mrs. Travilla replied.

"Where's Papa?" Elsie asked.

"In the library looking over some new books. Your father has always cared for books more than anything."

As they walked through the garden, Edward asked, "Well, what do you think of our flowers?"

"They're really beautiful," Elsie said. "And you have so many kinds. That's a lovely cape-jasmine, and look! There's a cactus I've never seen before. Mr. Travilla, I think you have more beautiful flowers than we have at Roselands," Elsie declared. Her admiration greatly pleased Edward, for he took intense pride in his garden.

At dinner, Elsie sat beside her father.

"I hope she hasn't given you any trouble," Horace said to Mrs. Travilla.

"On the contrary," the old lady laughed. "We have had a grand time together, and I hope you will bring her to see me again very soon."

After dinner, they all adjourned to the veranda where thick trees shaded the house from the day's heat and a small stone fountain bubbled gaily. But the adults' conversation

soon bored Elsie, and she slipped away to the library. A book on the table caught her eye, and she settled on a comfortable sofa in the corner of the room. Soon she was lost to everything around her as she read.

"So here you are, Miss Elsie," came Edward's pleasant voice. "We've been wondering where you were these last two hours. I should have guessed you are a bookworm like your father."

He sat beside her and took the book from her hands. "You can finish that later. I want you to talk to me."

"But Papa will be leaving soon, and it's such a good book," she said.

"No, he won't come to take you away. I've made a bargain to keep you here," he said gravely. "You see, we think there are more than enough children at Roselands without you, and so your Papa has given you to me."

"You're only joking, Mr. Travilla."

"Not at all." he continued with great seriousness. "Can't you see I'm in earnest?"

Although Elsie was teased often enough by her aunts and uncles and should have recognized Travilla's jesting, her father's affection was too fragile and her fear of losing him too strong. At the thought of leaving him, she felt panic overtake her, and with a little cry of alarm, she ran to the veranda and into her father's arms. Clinging to him as if for dear life, she sobbed, "Oh, Papa! Please don't give me away. I'll be good! I'll do everything you say! I'll —"

"Why Elsie, what do you mean?" Horace asked in perplexity. Then he saw Edward standing in the doorway, a sheepish look on his face.

"Mr. Travilla says that you've given me to him," Elsie went on in great fright.

"Nonsense, Elsie," her father said. "How can you believe that I'd ever give you away? Why, I'd rather sacrifice everything I have than part with you."

Elsie looked up and searched his face. What she saw there brought reassurance, and sighing deeply, she laid her head on his shoulder and said, "I am so glad, Papa."

At this point, Edward came forward and patted her shoulder. "I must say, Miss Elsie, that I hardly feel complimented. I'm vain enough to think I'd be the better — or at least the more indulgent — father. Won't you try me for a month, if your Papa consents?"

Elsie shook her head.

"I'll let you have your own way in everything," Edward urged again.

"I don't want my own way, Mr. Travilla. I know that it isn't always the best," Elsie said decisively, making Horace laugh and run his hand over her curly head.

"And I thought you liked me," Edward said in mock disappointment.

"I do like you, Mr. Travilla. Very much. I'm sure you'd be kind, and I'd love you, but never as much as I love my Papa. You're not my Papa, and never could be, even if he did give me away."

Horace laughed again and said to his friend, "I think you'd better give up, Edward. It seems I have to keep her after all, for she clings to me like a morning glory vine."

"Well, Elsie, will you at least come play a little for me at the piano?" Edward asked. But Elsie still clutched her father, until he loosened her grip and said in his forceful way, "Go on now, Elsie, and do as you are requested."

She rose instantly to obey. (Later Edward would complain to his mother, "I wish that Horace didn't always second my

requests with his commands. The child should be allowed to comply of her own will.")

Elsie sang and played until supper time, and afterward she sat quietly while her elders talked.

On the drive home to Roselands, Horace asked if she had enjoyed the day.

"Yes Papa, very much, except . . . . "

"Except what?" he asked, smiling down at her.

"Except when Mr. Travilla frightened me so."

"And do you really love your own Papa best? Are you sure you wouldn't exchange me for another?"

"Oh, no, Papa. Not for anybody in the world."

Horace didn't reply, though a gratified smile settled on his face, and they rode the rest of the way in a comfortable silence.

When they reached Roselands, Elsie kissed her father good night, and ran up the stairs to tell Chloe about her day.

"What a very pleasant visit we had," she said excitedly. "Papa was so kind, and so were Mr. Travilla and his mother."

"I'm glad, darling, and I hope you're going to have many more such days," Chloe said. As she undressed the child and prepared her for bed, Elsie regaled her nursemaid with a minute-by-minute account of everything that had occurred at Ion, even the terrible fright Edward Travilla had given her and its happy resolution.

"Well, you are mighty happy yourself, little girl," Chloe said.

"I am," Elsie agreed, "because I think my Papa is beginning to love me a little, and I hope he will soon love me very much."

The next afternoon, Elsie was returning from her walk when she met her father coming down the driveway. But instead of greeting her, Horace said sternly, "Elsie, I've forbidden you to walk out alone. Are you disobeying?"

"No, sir," she answered meekly. "I was with Aunt Adelaide and Louise until about five minutes ago. They said I was so near home I could come alone. They were going to make a call on a friend and didn't want me along."

Horace was somewhat mollified and took her hand. "How far have you been?" he asked.

"We went down the river bank to the big spring. I think it's about a mile that way, but we took a shorter way back, across the fields and through the meadow."

"The meadow?" Horace said, and he tightened his hold on her hand. "You are never to go into the meadow again, Elsie, unless you have my express permission."

"Why, Papa?" Elsie asked in some surprise.

"Because I forbid it," he said, "and that's enough for you to know. All you have to do is obey. You need never again ask why when I give you an order."

Elsie's eyes filled and a big tear rolled down her cheek. "I didn't mean to be naughty," she said, "and I'll try never to ask why again."

"Another thing, Elsie, you cry too easily. It's entirely too babyish for a girl your age. You must quit it."

"I'll try," she promised. She wiped her eyes and made a great effort to control her feelings.

As they approached the house, a little girl about Elsie's age came rushing out to meet them. "Oh, Elsie," she said

excitedly. "I'm so glad you've come. We've been here a whole hour — Mamma and Herbert and I — and I've been looking for you all the time."

"How do you do, Miss Lucy Carrington?" Horace said. "I see you can talk as fast as ever." He laughed and held out his hand.

Lucy shook it and replied with a little pout, "To be sure, Mr. Dinsmore, it hasn't been more than two weeks since you were at our house, and I wouldn't forget how to talk in just that short time." Then she turned to Elsie, clasping her friend around the waist. "We've come to stay for a week," she chattered, "and won't we have a fine time together?"

Elsie finally had a chance to speak, "I am glad you've come," she said sincerely.

"Is your father here, Miss Lucy?" Horace asked.

"Yes, sir, but he's going home tonight, and then he'll come back for us next week."

"Then I must go in and see him. Elsie, will you entertain Lucy?"

As her father walked away, Elsie suggested that the girls go to her room to play.

"Oh, yes, but won't you speak to Mamma first?" Lucy asked. "And Herbert, too? You're such a favorite with both of them. They're still in the dressing room because Mamma is not very well, and she's feeling tired from the ride."

Lucy led the way to her mother's room, babbling all the time. When they entered, Mrs. Carrington rose from the sofa and hugged Elsie close. "Elsie dear, how are you? I'm so glad to see you. I suppose you are very happy now that your father has come home. I remember how you always

looked forward to his return, constantly talking of it and longing for it."

Elsie wasn't sure what to say. Her father's return had not been as happy as she had always anticipated, but she didn't want to discuss it with Mrs. Carrington.

Luckily she didn't have to reply, because Herbert, Lucy's twin brother, came in at that moment and grabbed Elsie's hand. "I'm ever so glad to see you again, Elsie," he said, giving her hand a hearty squeeze. Elsie liked Herbert and felt sorry for him; he had suffered for several years from a hip condition that made him weak and sickly.

"Herbert always says that no one can tell such beautiful stories as Elsie," Mrs. Carrington chirped happily. "And no one except his mother and his nurse were so kind to him when he was bedridden here for so many weeks last year. Herbert has missed you very much, Elsie dear."

"How is your hip now, Herbert?" Elsie asked.

"Much better," the boy said cheerfully, though Elsie thought he looked very pale. "Sometimes I can take long walks now, but I can't run and leap like other boys. I still limp."

They all talked for awhile longer, then Elsie retreated to her room to dress for supper.

At the evening meal, Lucy, who was seated next to Elsie, took her third or fourth muffin and said, "These muffins are delicious! Don't you like them, Elsie?"

"Very much," Elsie said cheerfully.

"Then why are you eating cold bread? And you don't have any butter." Lucy turned to old Pompey and asked him to bring butter, but Elsie stopped him and then informed her friend, "I'm just fine, Lucy. And Papa doesn't allow me to eat hot breads or butter."

At this, Lucy's eyes opened wide, and she drew in her breath sharply. "I'm glad my Papa doesn't try that on me," she said. "Why, I'd make such a fuss he'd have to let me eat what I want."

"Elsie knows better than that," said Horace, who had been listening to the girls' conversation. "She would be sent from the table and punished for her naughtiness."

"I wouldn't do it anyway," Elsie said.

In an unusually kind voice, Horace replied, "No, Daughter, I don't believe you would."

The days of the Carringtons' visit passed very pleasantly. Lucy attended classes with Elsie in the mornings, though Herbert stayed with his mother. But in the afternoons, they all went out together, walking or riding. And if the weather was too warm, they played together on the veranda and then took their ride after sundown.

One afternoon, all the children were taking a walk — Arthur and Walter running far ahead because they would not accommodate Herbert's slow pace — when Herbert asked to stop and rest for awhile. "I want to try out my new bow, and you girls can pick up my arrows."

"Thank you, sir," Lucy laughed. "Elsie can chase your arrows if she likes, but I plan to take a nap. This soft grass will make an elegant couch." And she dropped onto the ground and was soon slumbering soundly, or pretending to be. Herbert shot his arrows here and there, and Elsie ran to retrieve them until she was hot and breathless.

"I have to rest," she said, sitting down beside Herbert. "What if I tell you a story?"

"Please do," said Herbert, laying down his bow. "You know how much I like your stories."

When she had finished her tale, Herbert took his bow again and sent an arrow sailing into the meadow.

"See how far it went!" he shouted happily. "Will you get it for me, Elsie?"

"This is this last time," she said, getting up reluctantly. Then she ran to where the arrow lay in the meadow, forgetting entirely her father's prohibition. She didn't remember until she had given the arrow to Herbert, and then in agitation, she exclaimed, "Oh, Herbert, I have to go home as fast as I can! I've forgotten! How could I forget? Oh, what will Papa say?"

"What on earth's the matter?" Herbert demanded anxiously, for Elsie's obvious distress alarmed him.

"Never mind," Elsie said, although she was crying now. "Look, the boys are coming back. They'll take care of you, and I must go."

She ran as fast as she could back to the house, sobbing all the way, and when she saw one of the servants, she asked where her father could be found.

"He's in the house," the servant answered, "but I don't know exactly where."

Before another word could be said, Elsie rushed inside and hurried from room to room. But Horace was not in the drawing room or the library. He wasn't in his own rooms. Elsie was just asking Fanny, the chambermaid, for help when her father's voice came from the veranda. "I'm here, Elsie," he called. "What do you want?"

Running outside, Elsie stopped when she saw her father, then approached him timidly. "I have to tell you something," she said, unable to control the quiver in her voice.

Horace could see that her face was flushed and tear-streaked. He took her hand and asked again, "What is it, Elsie? Are you sick? Have you hurt yourself?"

"No, sir, but — oh, Papa! I've been very naughty. I disobeyed you and went into the meadow!" With that, she burst into tears.

"How is that possible? Would you dare do what I positively forbade the other day?" Horace asked in his most severe voice.

"I didn't mean to disobey, Papa. I forgot you had forbidden me to go into the meadow."

"That is no excuse, no excuse at all. If your memory is so poor, I must find a way to strengthen it," he said.

He paused for a moment, looking at his sobbing, trembling child, then slightly softening his tone, he asked for an explanation.

"Tell me the whole story," he said, "so I may understand how to punish you."

Elsie gave him all the details of what had happened, and when he perceived that she really had forgotten and that her confession had been entirely voluntary, he relented. "Well, Daughter, I won't be very hard on you this time," he said calmly. "You seem very penitent, and you've made a full confession. But you must obey me, or next time you won't escape so easily. I do not take forgetfulness as an excuse. Now, go to Aunt Chloe and tell her to put you to bed immediately."

"But it's only the middle of the afternoon," she said.

"And that is your punishment. You are to stay in bed till tomorrow morning."

"But what will Lucy and Herbert think when they return and I'm not here?"

"You should have thought of that before you disobeyed," he said, a bit of gravity coming back into his voice. "Tell Chloe that you may have bread or crackers for dinner, but nothing more."

Elsie looked into his face. She seemed to want to speak but was afraid.

"Do you have something else to say?" he asked encouragingly.

"Yes, Papa. I'm so sorry for what I did. Will you forgive me, Papa? I won't be able to sleep if you're still angry with me."

Her sadness touched him more than he expected, and Horace said gently, "I do forgive you, Elsie. I am not at all angry with you now, so you can sleep in peace. Now good night, my child." And he kissed her lightly on her brow.

"Good night, Papa," she said with a little smile, "and I hope I'll never be so naughty again."

With his forgiveness, she went to her punishment. But once again, she found comfort in the pages of her worn Bible. She searched for some time before finding the verse she wanted in the twelfth chapter of Hebrews: "No discipline seems pleasant at the time, but painful. Later on, however, it produces a harvest of righteousness and peace for those who have been trained by it." Elsie recited the verse over and over to herself until she felt her hope renewed.

She rose early the next day and had learned all her lessons before breakfast. When she came down the stairs, she could see through the open front door that her father and several of the field hands were standing outside, gathered around some object on the ground.

"Come here, Elsie," her father said when she walked out onto the portico steps. He held out his hand, and she ran to him. He led her a few steps forward and pointed down. A large rattlesnake lay almost at their feet. The snake didn't seem to move, but it was ferocious looking nonetheless.

Elsie immediately jumped back and screamed, "Oh, Papa!"

"It's dead," he said, "and can't hurt you now. The men killed it in the meadow. Do you understand now why I forbade you to go there?"

Squeezing his hand tightly as she realized the danger, Elsie almost whispered, "I do, Papa. I might have lost my life by disobeying. Oh, how good God was to protect me."

Gently, her father said, "After this, I hope you always know that I have good reasons for my commands, even though I may not explain them to you."

"Yes, sir, I think I will," she said, still staring at the dead snake and imagining the possible consequences of her misbehavior.

———

At breakfast, Lucy finally got her chance to whisper to Elsie, "Where were you last night? I couldn't find you, and your Papa wouldn't tell me where you were, though I'm sure he knew."

Elsie blushed deeply. "I'll tell you later," she said quickly.

When the meal was ended, Lucy grabbed Elsie's waist, pulled her toward the veranda, and then said impatiently, "Now, tell me what happened. You promised."

Elsie's blush returned, climbing to the roots of her hair. "I was in bed," she said meekly.

"Before five o'clock!" Lucy exclaimed. "Whatever for?"

"Papa sent me," Elsie said with an effort, "because I was naughty and disobeyed him."

Lucy, who was always more full of curiosity than sentiment, demanded brightly, "Tell me what you did."

Shamed to recall her behavior, Elsie slowly explained, "Papa had forbidden me to go into the meadow, and I forgot all about it. I ran there to get Herbert's arrow."

"That's all?" Lucy declared in astonishment. "My Papa wouldn't punish me for something like that. He might scold me if I did it on purpose, but if I told him I'd forgotten, he'd just look at me a little sternly and say, 'You must remember better next time, my girl.'"

"My Papa says that forgetting is no excuse. He says that I must remember his commands, and if I forget, he has to punish me so I will remember better," Elsie said.

"He must be very strict, and I'm glad he's not my father," Lucy replied in a voice full of self-satisfaction.

But before Elsie could respond, Adelaide came to the door and called, "Hurry, girls. We are starting out in half an hour."

The whole family and their guests were going up the river for a picnic. They had been planning this excursion for several days, and the children were all looking forward to it a great deal.

"Did Papa say I can go?" Elsie asked, for she was not sure her punishment was ended.

"I presume you can, Elsie," her aunt said good-naturedly. "He never said you couldn't. But you girls must hurry now and dress, or you'll be late."

Just then, the library door opened, and Horace came out.

"Horace," his sister inquired, "Elsie is to go on the picnic, of course?"

"I don't see why you assume so, Adelaide," he replied dryly. "No, Elsie is to stay at home and attend to her lessons as usual."

Elsie's disappointment was sharp and showed in her face, but she didn't say a word and turned to go upstairs. Lucy, throwing a look of angry indignation at Horace, ran after her friend, and once they were in Elsie's room, Lucy declared, "It's not fair, and if I were you, I'd go on the picnic just to spite him!"

"I wouldn't do that," Elsie protested. "I must obey my father. God says so. And I couldn't go even if I tried, for Papa would know it and he'd stop me."

"Then you have to coax him," Lucy went on. "I'll come with you, and we'll talk to him together."

Elsie shook her head. "My father never breaks his word. Nothing would convince him after he has said I can't go." She was trying hard not to cry, but the tears came to her eyes as she told Lucy, "You have to go dress now, or you'll be too late."

Turning, but hesitant to leave her friend, Lucy said, "Alright, I'll go, but I won't enjoy myself without you."

Downstairs, Adelaide was just as indignant as little Lucy. "Why can't the child go with us?" she demanded of her brother. "I can't conceive of a reason you might have for keeping her here, and she is terribly disappointed. Indeed, Horace, I sometimes think you take pleasure in thwarting that child."

"So you think I'm a tyrant," he said sharply. "But I beg you to let me manage my child in my own way. And I have no obligation to explain my reasons to you or anyone else."

But Adelaide could not let the matter rest. "Well, if you didn't intend to let her go, you should have said so and not let the child build up her hopes. It's cruel."

His face now red with anger, Horace said, "Until this morning, Adelaide, I did intend to let her go on the picnic, and I intended to go myself. But I've just learned that I must meet a gentleman on an important business matter. You know as well as I how often accidents occur during these pleasure parties, and I'm not willing to send Elsie unless I am there to watch over her. Believe it or not, it's concern for her safety, not cruelty, that leads me to keep her at home."

His explanation just made Adelaide more impatient. "Honestly, Horace, you have such strange notions about that child. The rest of us will take care of her."

"No," he said adamantly. "If there's an accident, you will have enough to do taking care of yourselves. I won't trust Elsie with the group since I can't be there myself."

Seeing that her brother was determined to have his way, Adelaide gave up her attempt to dissuade him and excused herself. Elsie's disappointment was, of course, enormous, and for a good while, rebellion boiled inside her. She tried to put the feeling away, but it was strong. She couldn't imagine why her father refused to let her go on the picnic, except for yesterday's disobedience. It was unjust, she thought, to punish her twice, especially as she had confessed freely to him. It was a pity she hadn't heard his explanation to her Aunt Adelaide, for then she could have been content. But Elsie, though she sincerely desired to do right, was not perfect, and she had already forgotten the lesson of the rattlesnake.

Sadly, she watched the picnickers depart, all in the highest spirits, but she was surprised to discover that her father wasn't going with them. In a way, this helped reconcile her to her own fate. She didn't expect to see him that day, but it comforted her to know that he wanted her at home because he was there himself. Perhaps it was a selfish love, but it was better than none. (These were not Elsie's exact thoughts, of course. She would never have thought of calling her father selfish. Her feelings were not so defined as she watched him help the ladies into their carriage and then return to the house. What she felt was a troubling mixture of anger, disappointment, and confusion about her father's actions.)

It was a terrible morning for Elsie. Miss Day was in a dreadful mood. The teacher was secretly mortified that she had not been invited on the picnic, and her private misery made her more difficult and unreasonable than ever. Her incessant fault-finding and scolding were almost more than Elsie could bear, but at last the lessons came to an end, and Elsie was excused from the schoolroom. At dinner, there were only Elsie, her father, and the gentleman who had come to do business. The guest was not the kind of man who cared to notice children, so he and Horace discussed politics and business and paid no attention to Elsie.

She was very glad when her father finally excused her, but as she was leaving the dining room, he called her back. He explained that he had planned to ride with her that afternoon but could not do so after all. Jim would accompany her instead. Her father spoke so kindly that Elsie regretted her rebellious feelings. If they had been alone, she would have asked his forgiveness.

When Chloe was dressing Elsie for her ride, the little girl suddenly asked, "Is Pompey going into the city today?"

"Yes, darling, he's leaving pretty soon now."

"Then please do a favor for me, Aunt Chloe. Take some money from my purse and ask him to buy me a pound of the nicest candy he can find. I haven't had any candy for a long time, and I saw what they had bought for the picnic, and it looked so good."

When the Dinsmores and the Carringtons returned from their outing just before supper time, Lucy rushed to Elsie's room to tell her all about their delightful day. She gave every detail of their sports and entertainments, interrupting herself now and then to lament Elsie's absence as the only dark cloud over her pleasure. She repeated her assertion that Elsie's father was very unkind, and as she chattered, Elsie felt her own resentments rising again. She said nothing but allowed her friend to accuse her father of cruelty and injustice without any protest.

Lucy continued her narrative during supper, in a slightly more subdued tone, and Elsie asked questions until her father turned to her and said in his stern way, "Be quiet, Elsie. You are talking entirely too much for a child your age. Don't let me hear another word from you until you've left the table."

Elsie flushed hotly under his rebuke, but she uttered not a sound.

When they were excused, Lucy grabbed her friend and said, "Let's go into the garden and finish our talk. Your father can't hear us there."

"Papa only stopped us because we were talking too much at the table," Elsie apologized. "I'm sure he doesn't mind your telling me about your day." Then she lowered her voice to almost a whisper, "But please, Lucy, don't say again that you think Papa was unkind. I'm sure he knows best, and I never should have listened to any unkind words about him."

"Never mind then," Lucy said with good humor, and they skipped together down the path. "I won't say another word. But I do think he's cross, and I wish you were my sister and had my kind, good Papa for your own."

Elsie sighed. "I'd like to be your sister, but I wouldn't like to give up my Papa, for I love him so much."

"That's funny, when he's so cross to you!" Lucy exclaimed.

Elsie put her hand over Lucy's mouth, and Lucy pushed it away. "Excuse me. I forgot. I won't say it again," she laughed.

While the girls were in the garden, Fanny, the chambermaid, came onto the veranda where Horace was sitting and smoking a cigar. The young woman, who carried a small bundle, inquired if he had seen Elsie.

"What do you want with her?" he asked.

"Only to give her this package that Pompey brought from the city."

"Well, you can leave it with me," Horace said.

Meanwhile Elsie and Lucy had returned to the house and finding Pompey in the hallway, Elsie asked if he had gotten the candy. He told her he had brought some very delicious treats and given them to Fanny to deliver. Fanny, who had just come their way, said that Elsie's father had the candy, and at this news, Elsie turned away in disappointment.

Lucy, who wanted to see her friend happy, as well as to enjoy a share of the sweets, said, "Go ask him for it, won't you?"

But Elsie just sighed, "I think I'd rather do without."

Lucy, however, was persistent, and she coaxed Elsie for some time. But when Elsie still refused to approach her father, Lucy volunteered to go herself.

Elsie agreed, and Lucy, trembling a little in spite of her boastful claim that she was not afraid, found Horace on the veranda. Putting on a great show of confidence, she said, "Mr. Dinsmore, sir, will you please give me Elsie's candy? She wants it."

"Did Elsie send you?" he asked coldly.

Somewhat frightened by his manner, Lucy said yes.

"Then, Miss Lucy, please tell Elsie to come directly to me."

Elsie received this message with fearful uncertainty. But as she had no other choice, she went immediately to her father.

"Did you want me, Papa?"

"Yes, Elsie. I wish to know why you sent another person for what you want instead of coming to me yourself. It displeases me very much, and you will never get anything you ask for in this way."

Elsie hung her head and said nothing.

"Are you going to answer me?" he demanded. "Why did you send Lucy instead of coming yourself?"

"I was afraid," she said in the softest whisper.

"Afraid? Afraid of what?" he asked, and she could hear the displeasure growing in his voice.

"Afraid of you, Papa," she replied in a voice so low he could barely understand the words.

His anger rose, and he exclaimed, "If I were a drunken brute, if I were in the habit of beating you, there might be some reason for your fear. But as it is, I can see no excuse for it at all, and I am hurt and disappointed."

"I'm sorry, Papa," she said. "I won't do it again."

Then after a moment's pause, she said in a hesitating way, "Papa, may I have my candy, if you please?"

"You may not. And understand that I forbid you to buy or eat anything of the kind again without my express permission."

Elsie's eyes filled, and she choked down a sob as she slowly returned to Lucy. The two little girls sat close together on the steps of the portico.

"Have you got the candy?" Lucy asked eagerly.

Elsie shook her head.

Indignantly, Lucy raved, "It's a shame. He is just as cross as he can be! Why, he's a tyrant! That's what he is, a hateful, old tyrant! And I wouldn't care a cent for him, if I were you! I'm glad he's not my father!"

Elsie merely sighed and said, "I'm afraid he doesn't love me much. He hardly ever lets me have anything or go anywhere I want."

"Well, never you mind," Lucy said. "I'll send to the city tomorrow for *two* pounds of candy, and then we'll have a real feast!"

Sadder still, Elsie said, "Thank you, Lucy, but Papa has forbidden me to eat anything of the sort without his permission."

"He doesn't have to know about it," Lucy encouraged.

But Elsie shook her head again. "You're kind, but I can't disobey Papa, even if he never knows, because that would be disobeying God, and He would know."

Frustrated, Lucy could only lament, "You are very strange, Elsie."

To make matters worse, Horace approached the girls at that moment. From the doorway, he called, "Elsie, what are you doing out there? Haven't I told you not to go out in the night air?"

"I didn't know you meant the doorstep, Papa. I thought you meant the garden," she replied as she rose to go inside.

But Horace would not let her pass. "I see you intend to travel at the very edge of disobedience," he said harshly.

"Go straight to your room and have Chloe put you to bed."

Elsie silently obeyed, and Lucy started to follow, but Horace stopped her. "She is to go alone, if you please, Lucy," he said. And so the little girl, with a frown and a pout, turned on her heel and went to her mother in the drawing room.

Horace walked out onto the steps of the portico where he could watch the moon that was just rising above the tree-tops. But he was not to have this moment alone. From the shadow of a tree near the steps, Arthur sauntered forward and came to Horace's side.

"Elsie thinks you're a tyrant," Arthur began in a voice thick with snide conceit. "She says you never let her have anything or go anywhere and that you're always punishing her. She and Lucy had a fine time out here, talking about how badly you treat her and making plans to have candy behind your back."

"Arthur, I don't believe Elsie would deliberately plot to disobey me. And whatever faults she may have, I know she is above the meanness of telling tales," Horace replied. Then without a look at his younger brother, Horace turned and went into the house, leaving the crestfallen Arthur to creep away.

Chloe was not in the bedroom, for she hadn't expected to be needed so early and was down in the kitchen enjoying a chat. Elsie had to ring for her, and while the child waited, she reviewed in her mind the happenings of the day. She always did this before bed, but rarely was her retrospect so painful. Her tender conscience told her that she had more than once indulged in wrongful feelings toward her father. She had allowed Lucy to speak disrespectfully

of him, and by her silence, she'd given the remarks her own tacit approval. Worse, she had complained about him herself.

Tearfully, she murmured to herself, "How soon I forgot the lesson Papa taught me this morning and my promise to trust him without knowing his reasons. How can he love me when I'm so rebellious?"

"What's the trouble, darling?" Chloe asked as she came in. She took Elsie on her lap, cradling the child's head as she said, "I can't bear seeing you so upset."

"I've been so bad today, Aunt Chloe. I'm afraid I'll never be as good as Papa wants me to be. I know he's disappointed with me because I disobeyed him today," Elsie said, as her tears rolled down her cheeks.

"Then you must go to the throne of grace and tell the Lord Jesus about your troubles," Chloe said. "Remember what the Bible tells us: 'If anybody does sin, we have one who speaks to the Father in our defense — Jesus Christ the Righteous One.' Speak to Jesus, darling, and ask Him to help you trust your Papa and obey him even when you don't understand his reasons."

"You're right, Aunt Chloe. Jesus will forgive me and give me right thoughts and feelings," Elsie proclaimed. Then she wrapped her arms around her nursemaid's neck for a loving embrace.

She told Chloe of her father's directions and began to prepare for bed. She had stopped crying, but her face was still sad and troubled. When she was in her nightdress, with her hair brushed and tucked in her nightcap, Elsie took her little Bible and in a trembling voice, read from the twelfth chapter of Proverbs: "Whoever loves discipline loves knowledge, but he who hates correction is stupid."

"I must learn to be grateful for Papa's correction," she told herself, "but Jesus will have to help me." Sighing, she knelt by her bed and prayed. Chloe, watching her little girl, was filled with compassion, and she gave the child every assurance of her own love before tucking her into bed.

But for the next half hour, Elsie shifted and tossed.

"What makes you so restless tonight?" Chloe finally inquired.

"Oh, Aunt Chloe, do you think Papa might come and see me? There's something I must tell him. Would you go and see if he is busy? Don't disturb him if he is, but if not, will you ask him to come see me for just one minute?"

Chloe was not gone long, and she returned with the news that Horace was indeed busy with the guests. "You just go on to sleep, darling," the nurse soothed, "and you can tell your father all about it in the morning."

There was nothing left to try, and Elsie finally cried herself to sleep.

The next morning Lucy was at Elsie's door bright and early. "I was in a hurry to see you, Elsie," she explained. "This is our final day here, you know. Wasn't it too bad your father sent you to bed so early last night?"

"Papa has a right to send me to bed whenever he pleases. I was naughty and deserved to be punished, and besides, it wasn't much earlier than my usual bedtime."

"You, naughty?" Lucy exclaimed. "Mamma often says she wishes I were half as good as you."

Elsie said nothing, for her thoughts were far away. She was thinking of what she had wanted to tell her father and

gathering the courage to approach him this morning. "If I can get close to him when no one is near, and if he speaks kindly to me, then I can do it," she mumbled to herself.

"Can't you hurry, Aunt Chloe?" Lucy asked impatiently. "I want to run in the garden before breakfast."

Chloe, who had just re-tied Elsie's sash for the third time and smoothed the child's curls, laughed and said, "We're done now, but Elsie's Papa is very particular."

"He always wants me to look very nice and neat," Elsie explained. "When I go downstairs in the morning, he looks me over from head to toe. If anything is wrong, he's sure to notice and send me back to have it put right."

"You girls run along now and have a pleasant time before the bell rings," Chloe said as she tied the ribbon of Elsie's hat. "There, you look as sweet and fresh as a moss rosebud."

The girls skipped hand-in-hand out of the house and played in the garden until it was almost time for breakfast. Then Elsie went back to her room so Chloe could brush her hair smooth again. She had just rejoined Lucy in the front hall when they saw a carriage driving up to the front door.

"That's my Papa!" Lucy cried joyfully, and she ran straight to the arms of the gentleman who alighted from the carriage, receiving such hugs and kisses as Elsie had always longed for. Lucy was the Carringtons' only daughter and the apple of her father's eye, and Elsie watched this reunion with a strange ache in her heart.

But Mr. Carrington soon set Lucy down and turned to Elsie, taking her hand and giving her a warm kiss. "How are you this morning?" he asked her. "I'm afraid you can hardly welcome me, as I will be taking Lucy home. Have you two had a good time together?"

"Yes, sir, we have, and I hope you'll let Lucy come again soon."

"I certainly shall, but the visits mustn't be all on one side. I'll talk to your father and perhaps persuade him to let you return with us to Ashlands today."

"How wonderful!" Lucy said, clapping her hands. "Do you think he will let you, Elsie?"

"I don't know," Elsie said doubtfully. "I'm afraid not."

"Then you should coax him, as I coax my Papa."

Elsie simply shook her head, and they went to the break-fast room. Her father was there, but when she spoke to him, his reply was so cold and distant that she dared not say any-thing else. Horace hadn't intended to be influenced by Arthur's malicious tales, but unconsciously, he was. His atti-tude to his daughter this morning was colder than it had been in a long time.

After breakfast, Lucy reminded Elsie of her promise to show some beautiful shells her father had collected during his travels. The shells were kept in a curio cabinet in a small room off the library. Elsie knew that the items in this room, most of them belonging to her father, were rare and costly, and she was very careful of them.

But the girls were followed into the little room by Arthur, Walter, and Enna. Elsie, terrified of an accident, begged them to leave, but Arthur, declaring that he had as much right to be there as she, refused to budge. Instead, he gave Elsie a hard shove. Clutching at a small table to keep herself from falling, she dislodged a fine, old china vase that Horace prized dearly. It fell with a loud crash and shattered around their feet.

"Look what you've done!" Arthur shouted, and Horace, hearing the noise and the children's agitated voices, was soon on the scene.

"Who did this?" he demanded, looking from one child to the next.

"It was Elsie," Arthur said. "She threw it down and broke it."

Horace was angrier than Elsie had ever seen him. "You troublesome, careless child!" he yelled. "Go to your room immediately, and stay there till I send for you. And remember, if you ever come in here again without my permission, I promise you will regret it."

Elsie fairly flew from the room and up the stairs, and Horace rushed the other children out, slamming the door behind them.

In the hallway, Lucy turned angrily on Arthur. "How dare you blame it on Elsie? It was all your fault, and you know it, Arthur Dinsmore!"

"I didn't touch that old vase, and I'm not taking the blame, little miss," Arthur said threateningly. But coward that he was, he was all the while backing away from Lucy, with Walter and Enna close at his side.

For some time, Lucy was left to debate with herself: Did she have the courage to face Elsie's father and tell him what had really happened? At length, she resolved her dilemma in favor of her friend. Squaring her shoulders and holding her head high, she went back down the passage to the library. Horace was writing when she entered, and he looked up with an expression of surprise and not a little impatience.

"What do you want, Lucy?" he asked. "Speak up, for I am very busy."

"I just wanted to tell you," Lucy said boldly, "what really happened to the vase. Elsie was not at all to blame. It was Arthur. He pushed her hard and made her fall against the table, and that's how the vase fell."

"And why did he push her?"

"Because Elsie had asked him and Walter and Enna to leave. She was afraid they might do some mischief, and she was right."

Horace sat still for a moment, his pen suspended above his paper and his face clouded. But soon he turned to Lucy and said quite pleasantly, "Thank you very much, Miss Lucy, for your information. I would be very sorry to have punished Elsie unjustly. Will you do me the favor of telling her that her Papa says she need not stay in her room any longer?"

Lucy beamed with joy and relief, and she rushed away to her friend's room. Elsie was sobbing miserably when Lucy entered and delivered the good news. "So you don't have to cry or feel sorry for yourself now," Lucy concluded. "Dry your eyes, and we'll go down to the garden and enjoy ourselves."

Elsie was very grateful to Lucy and glad her father knew now that she wasn't to blame for breaking the vase. But his angry words had hurt her deeply, and though she tried to forget the incident and enter happily into Lucy's games, it would be a long time before the hurt was healed.

The girls played for much of the morning, then joined Mrs. Carrington in the drawing room. Herbert, who had not felt well enough to go outside, lay on the sofa with his head in his mother's lap. Horace and Mr. Carrington sat not far away, talking.

Lucy ran to her father and sat on his knee. Elsie, stopping first to say something to Herbert, nervously approached her own Papa and, with her eyes down, said softly, "I'm sorry about the vase, Papa."

Taking her hand, he drew her close and leaned forward to whisper in her ear, "Never mind that, Daughter. We'll forget about the vase. And I am very sorry that I spoke to you so harshly, since Lucy tells me you were not at fault."

His words brought great relief, but before Elsie could respond, Mrs. Carrington called out, "Elsie, we want to take you home with us to spend a week. Will you go?"

"I'd like to very much, ma'am, if Papa agrees," said Elsie, and she looked a little wistfully at her father.

"What do you say, Mr. Dinsmore?" Mrs. Carrington inquired. "I hope you have no objection." Then Mr. Carrington added, "By all means, you must let her come, Dinsmore. You can surely spare her for a week, and with Lucy's governess — a superior teacher, by the way — she can keep up with her lessons."

Horace looked grave, and before he said anything, Elsie guessed from his expression what his answer would be. Horace had several times noticed Lucy's disrespectful looks at him, and remembering the conversation reported by Arthur, he had decided that the less Elsie saw of Lucy, the better.

"Thank you both for your kind courtesy to my daughter," he said politely, "but while I appreciate your invitation, I must beg to decline. Home, I think, is the best place for Elsie at present."

With good humor, Mrs. Carrington said, "I suppose we should hardly expect you to spare her so soon after your return, but I am sorry. Elsie is such a good child, and I am always glad to have Lucy and Herbert with her."

"Perhaps you think better of her than she deserves," Horace said. "I find that Elsie is sometimes naughty and needs correction, just as other children. I think it best to keep her under my eye," he concluded, casting a serious look at his daughter.

Elsie flushed hotly and struggled not to cry. Fortunately the dinner ball rang, and Horace led her to the table. But she couldn't help thinking to herself how naughty her father would judge her if he knew about her thoughts and feelings of the day before.

As the Carringtons prepared to depart, Lucy retired upstairs to put on her bonnet. Elsie was ready to follow, but Horace took her hand and held her back. "Lucy will be down in a minute," he said. He did not let go of her hand, even when Lucy came back, and he didn't leave her side as the girls said their good-byes.

But as Horace was talking to Mr. Carrington, Lucy ventured to say under her breath, "I think he's mean not to let you visit."

In equally low tones, Elsie protested, "I'm sure Papa knows best, and I have been naughty. But I'd dearly love to go with you."

Horace didn't loosen his hold on Elsie's hand until the Carringtons' carriage had disappeared down the drive. Then he told her to come to him in the library in a half-hour's time. Seeing that he had frightened her, he added, "Don't be afraid. I'm not going to hurt you."

Elsie tried not to be afraid, but she had to wonder what he wanted, and despite her best efforts, she trembled a bit when she approached the library. He was alone there, sitting at a table covered with papers and writing material. Elsie saw his account book, and beside it a pile of bank notes and gold and silver coins.

"Come here, Elsie," he said, motioning her to the table. "I have your month's allowance. Your grandfather paid it to you in the past, but of course, it is my responsibility now. You have been receiving eight dollars, but now it will be ten."

He counted the money carefully and laid it before her. "From now on, I will require a strict accounting of everything you spend," he continued. "I want you to learn to keep accounts, for someday you will have a great deal of money to take care of. I've prepared an account book for you, so you can do it easily. Every time you spend or give away money, write it here as soon as you can. Be particular about doing it, so you don't forget anything. At the end of each month, you must bring your account book to me and let me see how much you have spent and what your remaining balance is. If you can't make it square, then you will lose part or all of your next month's allowance, according to the delinquent amount. Do you understand?"

"Yes, sir."

"Very good. Now, let's see how much you can remember of your last month's expenditures. Take your book and write down everything you remember spending."

Elsie had a good memory, and she was able to recall almost every penny. She wrote each number down, then added all the numbers in the column correctly.

"That was very well done," her father said with approval as he looked over the figures. "Let's see. A half a dollar for candy. Remember that you are not to buy candy anymore, not as a matter of economy, but because I think it injurious. I want you to grow up strong and healthy."

Suddenly, he closed the account book and asked her, "Were you very anxious to go to Ashlands?"

"I would have liked to go, Papa, if you'd been willing," she said meekly.

"I'm afraid Lucy isn't a good companion for you. I think she puts bad notions in your head," he said seriously.

Elsie flushed, and she was about to make her confession when the door opened and her grandfather entered. She kept silent.

"Doesn't Lucy sometimes say naughty things to you?" Horace asked in a low voice, so his father would not overhear.

"Yes, sir," Elsie replied.

"I thought as much. I shall keep you two apart as often as possible, and I hope there will be no grumbling from you."

"No, sir."

Then he put the allowance money in her hand and dismissed her. After she left, he sat and quietly contemplated. The list of Elsie's expenditures had consisted almost entirely of gifts for others, especially the servants. There were some beads and sewing silks for making a purse and a few drawing things, but with the exception of the candy, she had bought nothing else for herself.

"What a dear, unselfish, generous little thing," Horace thought. But he had not yet rid himself entirely of his old prejudices against his child. "I must not leap to conclusions," he told himself. "I can't judge from one month alone. She seems submissive, but perhaps that is for effect. I overheard her speaking to Lucy, but she may have suspected that I was listening. Perhaps she really does think I am a tyrant, and she obeys out of fear, not love."

This last thought — which, had he known, expressed his own fears more than his child's — came strongly and drove away the tenderness that had been warming his feeling.

New Rules

When he next met Elsie, his manner was as cold and withdrawn as ever, and Elsie could not bring herself to tell him what was in her heart.

CHAPTER

5

Gold Watch Mischief

*"A wise man fears the Lord
and shuns evil, but a fool
is hotheaded and
reckless."*

PROVERBS 14:16

Gold Watch Mischief

*O*ne hot afternoon, in the week after the Carringtons' visit, Arthur, Elsie, Walter, and Enna had just set out for a walk when Elsie spotted an object that instantly sent a cold chill through her. Catching the light of the sun, the object glittered brilliantly — a gold chain dangling from the pocket of Arthur's jacket.

Elsie immediately recognized it, for there was only one such heavy gold chain within Roselands. Taking her young uncle by the elbow, she whispered urgently, "Arthur! How could you take Grandpa's gold pocket watch? Please, put it back now. You're sure to break it otherwise."

Arthur jerked his arm from her grasp. "Hold your tongue, Elsie," he hissed at her. "I can do exactly as I want."

"But Arthur, you know that Grandpa would never let you take his watch. He's told us all how very valuable it is. He paid a lot of money for it, and he says it's worth even more than he paid."

Arthur turned on her. "If this watch is such a prize, then Papa shouldn't leave it lying around on his table." The boy leered hatefully into her worried face. "I'll just teach the old man a lesson, I will. It's about time he learned to be more careful with his things."

Elsie pleaded once more, "Please, take it back now, Arthur. If anything happens to that watch. . . . You know how angry Grandpa will be. Then he'll ask us all what happened, and you know I can't lie to him. He'll ask me if you took the watch, and I can't say no."

"Oh, you're a great little tattletale, Elsie Dinsmore," Arthur snarled. "But if you ever tell on me, I'll make you pay. Believe me, Elsie. You *will* be sorry."

Elsie's Endless Wait

His threat issued, Arthur ran ahead, down the dusty drive, with Walter and Enna trying to keep pace. But Elsie lingered behind them. She walked slowly, but her mind was in a whirl. What should she do? Arthur would pay no attention to her, and all the adults in the household were away, so there was no authority to whom she could appeal for help. Perhaps she should just turn around and go back to the house then and there. If she were not present when the inevitable disaster happened, then she could not be a witness to it. But her father had firmly told her to stay with the other children that afternoon. Besides, she had already seen Grandpa's watch in Arthur's jacket. Even if nothing too terrible happened to the watch, she still knew that Arthur had taken it.

Unhappily she quickened her steps to catch up with the other children. Then another idea struck her. There was a faint hope that she could convince Arthur not to do anything that would endanger the watch. He might even let her take charge of it while he played. Ordinarily, Elsie would have been too afraid even to touch her grandfather's valuable possession, but if she could protect it from Arthur, then she would gladly be responsible.

Their play that afternoon was far from pleasant for Elsie. When the boys weren't running her breathless, then Arthur was up to some antic that made her tremble for the safety of the watch. Though she asked him to let her guard it while he romped and tumbled, Arthur merely answered back with jeers and taunts.

"I'll do just as I please," he laughed at her. "I will not be ruled by *you*, Elsie."

Then it happened. Arthur was scrambling up a tree when his jacket snagged on a limb. As Arthur tugged to release the cloth, his pocket was up-ended, and the precious watch

fell, like a golden spark, to the hard ground. It hit with a thud and a sharp crack.

Elsie screamed, and Arthur, now pale with fear, clattered down from the tree and stumbled to where the watch lay.

Its crystal was shattered, and each broken bit of glass flashed at them in the sunlight. Gingerly, Arthur picked up the watch, and they all saw that its case was badly dented. They knew that it was damaged inside, too, for the delicate, little hands no longer moved.

Walter shouted at his brother, "Now see what you've done, Arthur!"

Enna whined, "What will Papa do?"

Elsie could only stare at the terrible mess that Arthur held in his shaking hand.

"All of you, hush!" the boy finally exclaimed. His voice quivered, but whether from fright or rage, it was impossible to say.

He glared at each of them in turn. "If any of you dares to tell about this," he said with defiance, "I'll make you sorry to the last day of your life. I promise I will. Do you understand?"

The smaller children cowered in silence, but Elsie spoke up. "Grandpa will know that *somebody* did it," she said. "He will blame somebody, and Arthur, you can't let an innocent person be punished for what you did."

"I don't care who gets punished!" Arthur exploded. "Just so Papa doesn't find out that I did it."

He turned on Elsie, narrowing his eyes to thin, dark slits. "Remember this," he said in a low and nasty voice. "If you dare to tell on me, little Elsie, I *will* make you pay."

Elsie stood firm. "I won't say anything, Arthur, unless an innocent person is blamed or I'm made to speak. But I won't lie for you then. I'll tell the truth."

Suddenly, Arthur put up his tight fists and lunged at the girl, but Elsie was too quick for him. She darted behind the tree, and before Arthur could grab for her again, she fled, running as fast as she could up the long, dusty driveway. The angry boy pursued, but before catching up to her, he apparently thought better of creating more trouble for himself. He quit the chase, and Elsie escaped into the safe haven of the house.

Careful not to be observed by any of the servants, Arthur managed to restore the pitifully damaged watch to its place on his father's table. Then he, Walter, and Enna gathered what courage they could to await their father's coming.

Arthur was not yet finished with his schemes. When he had calmed himself, he approached his little brother and took him aside. "I say, Wally," Arthur began in a voice as soft as butter. "You know my new riding whip?"

"Of course," said the smaller boy with interest.

"If I should give my new whip to you," Arthur asked, "what would you give to me in return?"

Walter's face lit up with his excitement. "Anything I've got," he almost shouted. Then his face fell. "You're just teasing me again. You'll never give me that whip."

"But I will give it to you," Arthur said agreeably, "if you'll be a good fellow and do what I tell you."

"What's that?"

"All you must do is to tell Papa that Jim broke the watch."

Astonished, Walter protested, "But Jim didn't do it! He wasn't even watching us. He was at the stables all afternoon."

"So what of it?" Arthur demanded with impatience. "Papa doesn't know where Jim was. He's just a slave anyhow. What do you care about him?"

"But I do care, and Jim will be punished," Walter said, "and I don't want to tell such a big lie."

"Then you won't get the whip. But if you don't do as I ask," Arthur went on, his voice becoming low and cold, "then I'm sure you will see a ghost one night very soon. There's one who comes to me sometimes, and I will send it to you."

The little boy cried out, "Oh, please don't do that, Arthur. I'm so afraid of ghosts." As he spoke, Walter looked nervously over his shoulder, half-expecting the dreaded haunt to appear at that very instant.

"If you don't do as I say, then I'll have the ghost come to your room tonight. Is that what you want me to do, Wally?" Arthur peered down at the terrified child, then he went on speaking even more softly, "You are a small boy yet, Wally. It would be easy for the ghost to carry you off. We'll probably never see you again."

Walter's eyes grew round, and his mouth fell open. Words tumbled out in a cascade of terror: "Don't, Arthur! Please don't send the ghost! I'll say anything you want me to say."

Arthur smiled. "That's a good boy, Wally. I knew I could trust you."

Arthur's terrible threat proved even more effective with little Enna, and she quickly promised to speak against Jim rather than face a ghostly visitor in the night.

Arthur could not try his tricks on Elsie. On returning to the house, she had gone directly to her room. For the remainder of the afternoon, she sat there in a state of terrible anticipation, waiting for the sound of footsteps that would signal a summons from her grandfather.

But the footsteps never came, and finally the dinner bell rang. When Elsie had nervously come downstairs and entered the dining room, she discovered, to her great relief, that her grandfather and Mrs. Dinsmore had still not arrived back at Roselands.

As Elsie slipped into the seat beside her father, Horace scrutinized his daughter's face. "You look pale," he said. "Are you well?"

"Yes, Papa, quite well."

Though Horace continued to study her with concern, he said no more, and when the evening meal was done, Elsie hurried back to her room.

It was not long before the elder Mr. Dinsmore and his wife returned. For once, they had brought no late-night visitors. They had not been in the house more than a few minutes when Mr. Dinsmore went to get his watch.

Grabbing up his shattered treasure, Mr. Dinsmore stormed into the drawing room. His suspicions had fallen immediately on Arthur, whose talent for mischief was well established at Roselands, and flushed with rage, the old man demanded, "Where is Arthur? Where is that young scoundrel?" Holding the battered watch out for all to see, he thundered, "This is some of *his* work, I've no doubt!"

In her smoothest tone, Mrs. Dinsmore said, "My dear, how can you say so? Do you have any proof? It's simply not fair to blame my poor boy for everything that goes wrong."

"He gets no more blame than he deserves," replied her furious husband. Bellowing, he called, "Arthur! Arthur, where are you?"

"He's in the garden, I think," said Horace. "I saw him walking there a few moments ago."

Mr. Dinsmore instantly sent one of the servants to bring Arthur inside. A second servant was dispatched to find the overseer of the plantation, and a third was ordered to assemble all the household and stables servants.

"I'll sift to the bottom of this," Mr. Dinsmore exclaimed, "and child or servant, the guilty person *will* suffer."

The old man was angrily walking the room when Arthur appeared. "How dare you meddle with my watch?" Mr. Dinsmore demanded of his son.

Arthur responded boldly. "I didn't, sir. I never touched it."

"There, my dear, I told you so," Mrs. Dinsmore declared in triumph.

"I don't believe him," said Mr. Dinsmore, then he turned his fiery eyes on his son. "Arthur, if you are guilty, as I strongly suspect, you had better confess at once, before I find the truth in some other way."

"I didn't do it, sir," Arthur lied. "It was Jim. Walter and Enna saw him, too. We all saw the watch fall from Jim's pocket when he was up a tree. He cried like anything when he found it broken, and said he didn't mean any harm. Jim said he only wanted to wear your watch for a little while and then put it back all safe. But now you'd find out and have him whipped."

"If what you say is true," the old man shouted, seeking out Jim's face among the servants gathered near the door, "I'll have him whipped and send him to work with the slaves in the fields. No such meddlers will stay in my house!"

Mr. Dinsmore looked at Enna. "What do you know about it?" he asked.

Glancing uneasily around the room, the little girl blushed and said, "It's true, Papa. I saw Jim do it."

"And you, Walter, did you see it, too?'

"Yes, Papa," the boy replied reluctantly. "But please don't punish Jim. I'm sure he didn't mean to break it."

"Hold your tongue!" the old man shouted with fury. "He *will* be punished!" Without asking any questions of Jim or hearing the young man's protests, Mr. Dinsmore pointed a shaking finger at the accused and ordered the overseer to "take him out now and give him a punishment that he will never forget!"

Alone in her bedroom, Elsie could hear nothing of the commotion below. She was trying to learn a lesson for the next day but found it very difficult to concentrate her thoughts. Suddenly, Aunt Chloe entered. She was clearly upset and held her apron to her weeping eyes.

"Oh, Aunt Chloe," Elsie said, "what's the matter?" In her alarm, Elsie dropped her book and ran to her nurse. "Has anything happened to you?"

"Not to me, little darling," Chloe sobbed. "It's Jim. He broke your Grandpa's gold watch, and now he's going to be whipped. Aunt Phoebe is crying fit to break her heart about her son, because —"

Elsie could hear no more. She ran into the hall, nearly colliding with her father. Bursting into tears, she exclaimed, "Papa! Oh, Papa! Don't let them whip poor Jim!"

"I cannot interfere," Horace said, trying to calm his distraught child. "Jim has done wrong and must be punished."

"But Jim didn't break the watch! I know he didn't because I saw it all!"

Much surprised, Horace asked, "Then who did break the watch, Elsie? It couldn't have been you, could it?"

"No, Papa! Not me. I never touched the watch. Please don't make me tell tales," she cried in great distress, "but it was not Jim! Please, Papa, stop them now, before he is whipped!"

Horace called out urgently to Aunt Chloe, "Go and tell my father to delay the punishment until I can speak to him. Tell him I will be down in a few minutes. Hurry!"

As the old nursemaid hastened down the stairs, Horace took Elsie's hand and led her back into her room. Drawing her to his side, he said, "If you want to save Jim, then Elsie, you must tell me all that you know."

The little girl pleaded again, "Don't make me tell tales, Papa. It's so mean. Isn't it enough for me to tell you that Jim didn't do it?"

"No, Elsie. It is necessary that you tell me all you know." He saw the tears flowing from her eyes, and he continued, speaking very kindly, "I would naturally be ashamed of you if, in ordinary circumstances, you were willing to tell tales on other people. But now it is the only way to save Jim. Unless you tell all you know, Jim will be severely punished and then sent away from this house. You understand how that will hurt his poor mother. Elsie, I think it would be wicked to let an innocent person suffer when you can prevent it. And as your father, I instruct you that you must obey me and tell the full truth now."

Elsie understood everything that her father was saying, and although reluctant, she did tell the whole story, her simple and straightforward words confirming her truthfulness for him.

The moment she finished, Horace took her hand and led her to the door. "You must repeat this story to your grandfather," he said.

Elsie pulled at his hand, wanting to retreat into her room. "Please, don't make me do it, Papa," she begged.

Sternly, Horace replied, "You must, my daughter," and he guided his child into the presence of her grandfather.

Except for Walter, the family were still gathered in the drawing room. Mr. Dinsmore, disturbed and angry, paced the room and cast occasional, mistrusting glances at Arthur. The boy, who had guessed the meaning of Aunt Chloe's message from Horace, was now the picture of guilt.

Walter had crept away from the scene. Crying over Jim's fate and his own lack of courage, the little boy told himself that he would make it up to Jim somehow — even if it cost a month's worth of allowance.

With Elsie's hand firmly in his own, Horace entered the drawing room and announced to his father, "I have another witness, sir. Elsie was there when your watch was broken."

"Then maybe I'll get the truth now," the old man exclaimed.

"It wasn't Jim, Grandpa. But please don't make me say who it was," Elsie cried.

Her father tightened his hold on her hand, and commanded, "Elsie! The whole truth now."

Elsie clung to his side and just caught a threatening look from Arthur. Horace, sensing her terror, also looked at Arthur and returned the boy's malicious gaze with his own hard stare.

Mr. Dinsmore addressed Elsie, "If you don't tell me what you know, child, then I can't let Jim off. Come now, Elsie. No one will hurt you for speaking the truth."

Sobbing, she blurted out, "I'll tell you, Grandpa, but please don't be angry with Arthur! Forgive him this time,

and he won't meddle anymore. I'm sure he didn't mean to break your watch."

Mr. Dinsmore was at his younger son's side in an instant. He seized the boy by the shoulder and raged, "I knew it had to be you!" Holding Arthur securely, he turned back to Elsie. "Let's have the rest of the story, little girl," he demanded.

When she had finished, Arthur began to plead for his father's forgiveness.

"Forgive you?" the old man spluttered. "I'll forgive you — after you have had a good spanking and a week of solitary confinement with nothing but bread and water!"

He was about to drag Arthur from the room when Elsie rushed to his side. "Please, don't punish him, Grandpa! He won't do it again, will you Arthur? And let me pay for the watch. I *want* to pay for it."

"I don't care about the money," her grandfather replied, a hint of contempt in his voice. "And where would you get that kind of money?"

"But I'm rich, aren't I?" she said softly. "Didn't my mother leave me a great deal of money?"

Her father gently took her to his chair. He sat down and held her before him. "No, Elsie," he explained. "Until you come of age many years from now, you have only what I choose to give you."

"Then please, give me the money for the watch, Papa."

"I can't do that, Elsie. Arthur must take the penalty for his own wrongdoing," Horace said firmly. "That is what your grandfather cares about, not the money."

At this point, the elder Mr. Dinsmore harshly dragged Arthur from the room — but not before the boy had shot a burning look of hatred and defiance at Elsie. She felt his

intensity so deeply that she could hardly stand. Her father, seeing the exchange that had just taken place, steadied her and said soothingly, "Don't be afraid, Daughter. I will protect you."

It seemed to Elsie that her father was, at long last, about to lift her onto his knee, as he so often did with Enna, and to hug her close to him. But at that moment, a servant entered to announce the arrival of visitors, and Elsie was dismissed to her room.

As Elsie reluctantly left her father to his guests, she saw Mrs. Dinsmore, who plowed down the hallway like a massive ship in a storm; her face was grim and full of fury. Wanting to avoid any meeting with the woman, Elsie ran up the stairs to find solitude in her own quiet bedroom. But the room wasn't empty. Chloe awaited her. Aunt Phoebe was there too, and the woman's fervent expressions of gratitude made Elsie forget for the time that she wouldn't see her father again that night.

There was a knock at the door, and Jim put his head in. Elsie invited him inside and received his grateful thanks as well. Jim explained that he had been so astounded by the unexpected charges against him that he'd been unable to speak up in his own defense. Besides, Mr. Dinsmore had refused to listen to his protests of innocence. If it hadn't been for Elsie, well, no one wanted to contemplate what might have happened.

When Jim and his mother had gone and Chloe had settled down to her knitting, Elsie at last had time to think again of all that had happened. She remembered the understanding and kindness of her father that night, his loving words, and his protection and care. Bedtime came, and although she retired at precisely the time her father dictated, Elsie lay

awake for some time, imagining — as she had done so often before — a future in which her father would truly love her as much as she loved him.

At breakfast the next morning, she greeted Horace with an eager yet shy, "Good morning, Papa."

His response was both serious and absent-minded. Immediately beginning a business conversation with his father, Horace paid no further heed to his child, except to supervise the food that she was allowed to eat. When the meal was done, Elsie lingered at the table, hoping for her father's attention. But beyond a brief glance in her direction, there was none. Horace informed his father that he would be riding to Ion, to see Mr. Travilla, and probably would not return before night. Sadly disappointed, Elsie returned to her room to prepare for her morning lessons.

For awhile, Elsie enjoyed complete freedom from Arthur's torments. Even when his punishment was ended, Arthur was much too afraid of his brother Horace to openly bother Elsie in any way. In secret, however, he nursed his desire for revenge.

Aunt Adelaide was always kind; Lora still stood up for Elsie when she saw an injustice; and Elsie's grandfather was nice enough in his gruff fashion. But the rest of the family did little to make her feel comfortable. Mrs. Dinsmore remained extremely angry with her because of Arthur's disgrace, and when Horace was not around, the woman treated Elsie most unpleasantly. The younger children were unusually cold and distant. Even her father, though careful to see that all her wants were met, seldom seemed to take much

notice of her, unless to chide her for some fault. Nothing she did was too trifling to escape his eye.

One day, when Horace had sent Elsie to her room for some small thing, Adelaide said to him, "You seem to expect that child to be a great deal more perfect than any grown person I know. She is not even nine years old, yet you want her to understand all the rules of etiquette."

"If you please," he responded haughtily, "I would like to manage my own child as I see proper, without any interference."

Adelaide answered him calmly. "I had no intention of interfering. But really, Horace, you have no idea how eagle-eyed you are for any fault in Elsie, nor any idea how stern your tone is when you correct her. Remember that you have not been a father to her for more than a few months, and until you came home, she had never had a real parent before. But I've known Elsie for more than four years now; I've seen how sensitive she is and also how much she wants to do right and to please you. I'm sure that a gentle reproof would be just as effective and not hurt her feelings so."

"Enough!" Horace exclaimed impatiently. "Perhaps if I were ten years younger than you, instead of the other way round, you might be right to advise and direct me. But as it is, I regard your words as simply impertinent." With that, he angrily left the room.

Adelaide watched him depart and thought to herself, "I am glad you have no authority over me, dear brother."

All that Adelaide said was true; still, Elsie never complained or blamed her father. Indeed, in her heart she blamed herself for his cool aloofness. His many reproofs only made her more timid and sensitive, and she tended increasingly to distance herself from him. She seldom ventured to speak or even move in his presence, and she was far too young to understand that her behavior flowed naturally from his. As for Horace, he could plainly see that Elsie feared him. But prideful as he was, he was unable to admit the wisdom of Adelaide's words, so he attributed his daughter's reticence solely to her lack of love for him. And in this way, both father and daughter continued to walk their separate paths.

CHAPTER

6

Bird on the Wing

"Are not two sparrows sold for a penny?
Yet not one of them will fall to the ground
apart from the will of your Father.
And even the very hairs of your head
are all numbered.
So don't be afraid; you are worth
more than many sparrows."

MATTHEW 10:29 – 30

t was the Sabbath morning, and Adelaide, Lora, and Enna were already in the carriage. Elsie stood on the portico steps, waiting for her father, and watched as the horses, two young steeds purchased by Horace only a few days before, stamped and tossed their heads.

As Horace came out, he remarked to Ajax, the coachman, "I didn't intend to harness that pair today. Where are the old bays?"

"Old Kate has a lame foot, sir, and your father said these youngsters have to be put to use sooner or later. I reckoned I might as well take them out today."

Horace, glancing first at the horses and then at Elsie, asked, "Are you sure you can hold them in?"

Smiling broadly with self-confidence, Ajax said, "I've driven these horses twice already, and they went splendidly. I reckon I can hold them in good as anything, sir."

Still uneasy, in spite of Ajax's assurance, Horace turned to his daughter. For a moment, he considered keeping her home from church that day, but he realized what disappointment this would cause her, so he lifted her into the carriage, and ordering Ajax to proceed with caution, Horace climbed in and sat beside his child.

"Change seats with me, Elsie," Enna said, sounding very much like her mother. "I want to sit next to my brother."

But Horace, putting his hand on Elsie's shoulder, said, "No, Enna. Elsie's place is beside me."

Enna started to pout. Horace, however, turned his attention to Adelaide who asked him a little anxiously, "Do you think there's any danger of the horses bolting?" She had

seen Horace's concern, and she also realized that they were moving unusually fast.

"The horses are young, but Ajax is an excellent driver," Horace replied evasively. "Besides, I wouldn't have brought Elsie if I believed we were in any danger."

And in truth, their journey to church was uneventful. On the ride home, however, the horses took fright, and the carriage careered down a hillside at a frightful speed. Elsie thought they were going very fast, but she didn't suspect any danger until her father lifted her from her seat and placed her between his knees, holding her very tightly as if afraid that she might be snatched from his grasp. Elsie saw that his face was very pale and his eyes were fixed on her.

She whispered, "Don't worry, Papa. God will take care of us."

"I'd give all I'm worth to have you safe at home," he said hoarsely and held her even closer to him.

As their speed increased, the carriage bounced and shuddered and seemed ready to tip over at any second, an outcome they had little hope of surviving. Lora was leaning back in her seat, white with terror. Adelaide clutched Enna to her, and the little girl sobbed bitterly. But even in the face of death, Elsie remembered that they were in their Heavenly Father's hands. Her faith was strong, and she put her trust in Jesus.

As Ajax struggled to regain control over the charging horses, a large and powerful man, who happened to be walking down the road, heard a roaring, thudding sound behind him; he turned to see the galloping horses and imperiled carriage. Without a thought to his own danger, the man planted himself in the middle of the road, and as the horses neared, he reached out and grabbed their bridle — a

sudden check that caused the horses to rear excitedly and then halt.

"Thank God, we're saved!" Horace exclaimed. He threw open the carriage door and leaped to the ground, lifting Elsie out first and then his sisters. They were near the entrance to Roselands, and they all preferred walking the rest of the way to returning to the carriage. As Adelaide led her sisters to the house, Horace, keeping Elsie at his side, remained some time, thanking and talking with the man who had, at the risk of his own life, saved theirs. Although Horace insisted the man accept a handsome reward, he knew it could never be enough for the courageous rescue.

Ajax guided the horses back to the stable as Horace and Elsie walked slowly up the drive. Neither spoke a word until they reached the house; then Horace bent and kissed his child and asked if she had recovered from her fright.

"Yes, Papa," she said softly. "I knew that God would take care of us."

"That He did," Horace replied, very seriously. "Now go upstairs and tell Chloe to get you ready for dinner."

Later that afternoon, Elsie was alone in her room when Lora surprised her by entering. It was seldom that the older girls chose to visit their young niece.

Lora still looked a little pale, and more thoughtful than Elsie could remember. Lora didn't say anything at first, then suddenly she burst out, "Oh, Elsie! I can't help thinking, what if we'd all been killed? Where would we all be now? Where would I be? I believe you would have gone straight to heaven, but I? I would be like the rich man the minister talked about this morning, lifting up my eyes in torment."

Lora covered her eyes and a shudder ran through her. Then she said, "We were all so afraid, but you, Elsie. What kept you from being afraid?"

"I was thinking of a Bible verse I know. 'Even though I walk through the valley of the shadow of death, I will fear no evil, for you are with me.' God said for us not to be afraid because He is with us. I knew that Jesus was there with me, and if I were killed, I'd wake up again in His arms. That's why I wasn't so afraid."

"I'd give anything to feel as you do," Lora sighed. "But didn't you feel afraid for the rest of us? I'm sure you must know that even though we go to church and study the Bible sometimes, we are not very good Christians and don't even pretend to be."

Elsie blushed and looked down. "It happened so quickly I only had time to think of Papa and myself. I've prayed so much for Papa, and I was sure God would spare him. It was selfish, I know, and I can't tell you how thankful I was that we were all spared."

"You did nothing wrong," Lora maintained. "And we haven't given you much reason to care what becomes of us. But Elsie, can you tell me how to be a true Christian? I want to try very hard and never rest until I am one."

Elsie was overjoyed, and she picked up her little Bible. "Let me show you Jesus' words," she said, finding the verse she wanted. "'For everyone who asks, receives; he who seeks, finds; and to him who knocks, the door will be opened.' That must encourage you.

"And see this verse: 'You will seek me and find me when you seek me with all your heart.' Oh, dear Lora, all you have to do is seek Him. The Bible promises that if you seek the Lord with all your heart, you will find Him."

"Yes," Lora said a little doubtfully, "but how do I seek Him, and what must I do to be saved?"

Elsie, who knew the Bible more thoroughly than most children her age, recalled the answer that Paul the Apostle gave to the jailer: "'Believe in the Lord Jesus Christ, and you will be saved.'" She turned to the tenth chapter of the book of Romans and read aloud: "'If you confess with your mouth, 'Jesus is Lord,' and believe in your heart that God raised Him from the dead, you will be saved.'

"You see, Lora," said Elsie, "you simply have to believe in Jesus. But you must believe with your heart — not just your mind."

"But how do I get rid of my sins? How do I make myself pleasing in the sight of God?" Lora asked eagerly.

Elsie turned to the book of First John. "See what it says here, Lora?" she asked. "'The blood of Jesus Christ, His Son, purifies us from all sin.' Jesus has already done all that is necessary. We have nothing to do but to believe in Him and accept His offer of forgiveness of sins and eternal life. Just accept them as free gifts, and then love and trust Him."

"But surely I must *do* something?" Lora asked.

Elsie thought carefully. "Well," she replied, "God says, 'Give me your heart.' You can do that. You can invite Him to come live in your heart. You can tell Him how much you need Him. And the Bible says, 'If we confess our sins, He is faithful and just and will forgive us our sins and purify us from all unrighteousness.' So you can tell Jesus your sins and ask Him to forgive them. You can ask Him to teach you to be sorry for your sins and give you a desire to be like Him — loving and kind and forgiving. Of course, we can't be like Him without the help of His Holy Spirit. But we can always get that help if we ask.

"Oh, Lora, don't be afraid to ask. Don't be afraid to come to Jesus. But you must come humbly, for the Bible says 'God opposes the proud, but gives grace to the humble.' He won't turn away anyone who comes to Him humbly, seeking to be saved."

For the rest of the afternoon, Lora stayed with Elsie, asking questions and reading from the Scriptures. Elsie explained that being a Christian meant having Jesus in your heart, not just attending church and reading the Bible. Then they sang a hymn together, and Elsie talked about her own peace and joy in believing in Jesus. "Oh, how good of God to make being saved so easy that anyone can do it — even children like us," she exclaimed.

When the supper bell rang, Elsie went to join the others with a new sense of happiness. Besides the joy of her conversation with Lora, she also remembered her father's deep concern for her during their perilous ride. "Surely he does love me," she murmured to herself.

When Horace met her at the table and asked with a smile, "How is my little daughter this evening?" her cheeks glowed, and she wanted to throw her arms around him and tell him how much she loved him. That was impossible for her, with all the family gathered around, so she simply returned his smile and said, "I'm very well, thank you, Papa."

But once again her joy was short-lived, and before the week was out, she was again in sad disgrace.

It was a bright afternoon several days later, and Elsie was walking alone in the garden when she heard a fluttering

noise coming from a nearby arbor. Hurrying toward the source of the sound, she discovered an up-turned glass vase in which a beautiful hummingbird was imprisoned. Struggling to escape, the tiny bird fluttered and beat its fragile wings against the glass, causing the noise Elsie had heard.

Always tenderhearted, Elsie could never bare to see any living creature in distress. She knew that Arthur was often guilty of torturing insects and small birds — she'd several times endured his wrath to intervene on behalf of his small victims — so she instantly assumed that this was his handi-work. The desire to release the terrified bird overwhelmed her, and without a moment's hesitation or reflection, she lifted the glass, and the bird flew free.

Only then did she consider how angry Arthur would be, and the prospect caused a little shiver to pass through her. But it was too late now, and after all, she didn't really fear any consequences since she was sure her father would approve of her action. She'd often enough heard Horace reprove his brother for his cruel practices.

The day was very hot, and Elsie retreated to the veranda off the drawing room on the east side of the house, where a canopy of trees and vines provided cooling shade. Arthur, Walter, and Enna were just inside, enjoying a lively game of jacks, and Louise was stretched languidly on the couch, engrossed in her latest novel.

Elsie, taking up a book of her own, wondered why Arthur didn't go to check on his captive bird, but she soon forgot all about her uncle as she buried herself in the adventures of the Swiss Family Robinson.

The players were just finishing their jacks game when Horace suddenly burst into the room and demanded, in a

voice full of rage, to know who had been in the garden and released the hummingbird he had taken such pains to capture. It was one of a rare species, he said, and an important addition to his collection.

Elsie was terribly frightened and would have been glad to sink through the floor at that moment. She dropped her book, and her face turned pale and flushed in turns as she struggled to choke out a confession, as her conscience told her she must.

Her father's attention was focused not on her, but on Arthur. "I presume it was you," Horace was saying angrily, "and if I'm right, you should prepare yourself for punishment as severe as your last."

"I didn't do any such thing," Arthur replied with fierce indignation.

"Of course, you'll deny it," Horace went on, "but we all know that your word is good for nothing."

At that moment, a small voice interrupted the brothers' angry exchange.

"Arthur didn't do it, Papa. It was I."

"You?" her father exclaimed, turning on her an expression that oddly mixed anger and astonishment. "You, Elsie? Can this be possible?"

Covering her face with her hands, Elsie burst into tears.

"Come here to me this instant," Horace commanded. He took a seat on the settee that Louise had abandoned. "Tell me what you mean by meddling in my affairs."

"Please, please, don't be so angry, Papa," she sobbed, moving to him. "I didn't know it was your bird. I didn't mean to be naughty."

"You never *mean* to be naughty," he said. "Your misbehavior always seems to be by accident. But I find you are a

very troublesome and mischievous child. Remember the valuable vase you broke the other day, and now you've caused the loss of a rare specimen that I spent a great deal of time to procure. Really, Elsie, I'm tempted to administer a very strong punishment. Tell me why you did it. Was it pure love of mischief?"

"No, sir," Elsie said in a whisper. "I was sorry for the little bird. I thought Arthur put it there to torture it, so I let it go. I didn't mean to do wrong, Papa, really I didn't," she pleaded, her tears falling faster than ever.

"You had no business to meddle, no matter who put it there," he said. "Now, show me which hand did it."

Elsie held out her right hand, and Horace took it in his. He could feel her trembling, and when he looked into her face, he saw her fear and pain. The evidence of her sorrow relaxed his anger, and the stern expression faded from his face. He was tempted at that instant to forgive her entirely. But the loss of the rare bird was extremely upsetting, and his anger flared again. She must be punished, he decided, but not with physical pain. He freed his hand from hers and began to reach into his pocket.

"Watch out, Elsie," Louise laughed maliciously. "He's reaching for his knife. I expect he wants to cut off your hand."

"Hush, Louise," her brother said sharply. "I'd as soon cut off my own hand as my child's. You should never speak anything but truth, especially to children."

"I think it's sometimes good to frighten them a little," Louise replied defensively. "And I thought that's what you intended to do."

"Never," Horace said firmly. "That is a very bad approach, and one I'll never adopt. Elsie will learn in time,

if she doesn't know now, that I never utter a threat which I do not intend to carry out. And I never break my word."

While remonstrating with his sister, Horace had taken a linen handkerchief from his pocket. Lifting Elsie's hand again, he said to her, "I shall wrap up this hand, for those who do not use their hands aright should be deprived of their use. There!" He finished knotting the handkerchief, making sure it was not too tight. "Now go to your room and stay there till supper." He gave her a little pat on the back and sent her off.

Elsie felt deeply humiliated, so Arthur's nasty laugh and Enna's smug little smirk added nothing to her suffering. Her father's punishment, which was indeed mild, had wounded her more than the most severe chastisement, because the mere knowledge of his displeasure was the worst pain she could endure.

Walter, whose heart was much kinder than his brother's or sister's, was touched by Elsie's distress, and he ran after her when she had left the room. "Never mind, Elsie," he said sincerely. "I'm so very sorry for you, and I don't think you were the least bit naughty."

She thanked him, for she was deeply grateful for his concern. Then she hurried to her room. Alone, she sat by the window, and through her tears, she tormented herself with questions. "Why am I so naughty? How can I be good so that Papa will love me?" And she raised an earnest prayer for help to do right and for the wisdom to understand how to gain her father's love.

When the supper bell rang an hour later, Elsie jumped up, but then she sat down again. Better to have no supper, she decided, than to show her handkerchief-bound hand and tear-swollen eyes at the table. It was not long, however,

before a servant came to her door with a message from her father; she was to come down to the dining room immediately.

When she took her seat beside him at the table, Horace turned hard eyes on her. "Didn't you hear the bell?" he inquired.

"Yes, sir."

"Remember, Elsie, that you are to come as soon as you hear the bell, unless you are directed otherwise or you are sick. The next time you're late, I will send you away without your meal."

"But I don't want to eat," she said softly.

"Nevertheless, you will have your supper tonight, and there will be no pouting or sulking." His voice was low, but clearly irritated as he added, "Stop that crying at once." He spread some preserves on a slice of bread and laid it on her plate, and repeated, "Stop crying, or I'll take you from the table, and you will be very sorry."

Elsie was struggling valiantly to choke back her tears when her grandfather addressed her. "Why is your hand bandaged, little girl?" he asked. "Have you been hurt?"

Elsie's face flushed, but she said nothing.

"You must speak when you are spoken to," her father commanded. "Answer your grandfather's question now."

"Papa tied it because I was naughty," she said, a sob escaping with her words.

Horace made a move as if to take her away from the table, but Elsie begged him, "Please, don't, Papa. I'll be good."

"Then no more crying," he said. "This is shameful behavior for a girl of nearly nine. It would be bad enough for a child of Enna's age." He took a fresh handkerchief from his pocket and wiped her eyes. "Now eat your supper at once, and don't make me have to correct you again."

Elsie tried to eat her bread and jam, but it was almost impossible. Struggling as hard as she could to stifle her tears and sobs, she could not swallow and felt as if she might suffocate. She knew that her father was watching her closely, and she sensed that everyone else was looking at her. "If they would just forget about me," she thought.

It was at that moment that Adelaide, who had watched the whole scene, addressed a question to Horace and adroitly set the whole table talking about something else. How grateful Elsie was to her aunt for this time to regain her composure.

When they rose from the table, Elsie timidly asked if she might go to her room.

"No, child," her father said. Taking her left hand, he led her to the veranda. Horace settled in a comfortable chair and lit a cigar. He told Elsie to get his book from the drawing room; then he had her draw a stool close to his chair and sit beside him.

"Do not move from that stool. Let's see if I can keep you out of mischief for an hour or two," he said, and he began reading to himself.

"May I get a book to read, Papa?"

"You may not. Do just as I tell you, nothing more and nothing less."

Elsie took her seat on the stool and tried to amuse herself with her own thoughts. She watched her father's face as he read. "How handsome my Papa is," she thought. But her sadness came back to her again as she tried to decide how she could please him and win his love. More than anything, she wanted only to climb on his knee, hug him, and tell him how sorry she was about the bird. In her imagination, she could see him returning her affection with his own hugs and smiles.

A cry from Enna broke into her dream, and without thinking, Elsie jumped up from the stool. "Papa," she exclaimed, "there's a carriage coming up the drive. If it's visitors, please let me go to my room!"

"Why do you wish to go?" he asked coolly.

Elsie blushed and hung her head. "Because I don't want them to see me, Papa," she answered.

"You are not usually so afraid of strangers," he observed.

"But they will see that my hand is tied and ask me why. Oh, please let me go, Papa, before they get here," she pleaded desperately.

"No, you must stay, if only to punish you for leaving your seat without my permission. You must learn to obey me at all times, Elsie, and under all circumstances. Now sit down, and don't move again until I say you may."

Elsie sat quickly, but two hot tears dropped on her cheeks.

"You need not cry," her father said. "The visitor is only an old gentlemen here to see your grandfather on business. He never notices children, so he's not likely to ask you any questions. I really hope, Elsie, that you will learn to save your tears for an occasion that requires them."

Her father was right. The old gentleman paid no attention to her, and her relief was so great that, for once, she scarcely noticed Horace's rebuke. A half hour at least passed in silence, and Elsie grew so weary that without intending to, she laid her head on her father's knee and slept.

His voice seemed to come to her from far away. "You may go to bed now, Elsie, if you like."

She stood up slowly and was turning to go, but she hesitated.

"Do you have something else to say?" Horace asked.

"Yes, Papa. I'm sorry I was naughty today. Will you forgive me?" Her words were spoken softly, but she managed not to cry again.

Horace responded sternly, "In the future, will you try not to meddle in the affairs of others and not to sulk and pout when you are punished?"

"I will try to be a good girl always," she promised.

"Then I forgive you," he said, and he carefully untied the handkerchief and removed it from her hand.

But she still lingered, hoping for some token of his forgiveness. Sensing what she wanted, Horace considered what to do. With a hint of impatience, he said at last, "No, Elsie, I will not kiss you good night. You have been entirely too naughty. Now go straight to your room at once."

Could she *ever* win her father's love? The wait seemed endless at times. In her bed that night, Elsie searched her little Bible for words of hope. And she found them in the promise of God's eternal love: "For I am convinced that neither death nor life, neither angels nor demons, neither the present nor the future, nor any powers, neither height nor depth, nor anything else in all creation, will be able to separate us from the love of God that is in Christ Jesus our Lord." Whatever else happened to her, God's love would be with her always.

CHAPTER

7

A Terrible Injustice

"Consider it pure joy, my brothers, whenever you face trials of many kinds, because you know that the testing of your faith develops perseverance. Perseverance must finish its work so that you may be mature and complete, not lacking anything."

JAMES 1:2 – 4

A Terrible Injustice

*E*ach month, Miss Day presented the parents with reports on the conduct and recitations of her pupils. Horace Dinsmore had received one such report since his return to Roselands. It had been most satisfactory, as Elsie was usually a diligent scholar who tried to carry her religious principles into her studies as in everything else. As much as Miss Day looked for faults, Elsie's work rarely gave her good excuses.

Horace had pronounced the first report quite good. "I'm glad to see that my daughter is industrious and well-behaved," he had told Miss Day, "for I want her to grow into an intelligent and amiable woman."

Now the time for the second report arrived, and Elsie knew it would not be as the first. The warm weather of the last month had distracted her, and more seriously, she had often been too depressed and anxious to concentrate fully on her lessons. Arthur had become more annoying than ever; in the schoolroom he was forever shaking Elsie's chair and jogging her elbow when she was writing. Her copybook was very messy as a result, and Miss Day's report on her work had never been so bad. With secret satisfaction, the governess presented the report to Horace, together with a long list of complaints about the child's idleness and inattention.

"Send her to my room immediately," Horace said angrily.

Elsie was still in the schoolroom, putting her desk in order, when Miss Day brought the message. With a hateful smile, she said, "Elsie, your father wishes to see you this moment. He is waiting in his room."

Elsie's Endless Wait

The look on Miss Day's face told Elsie what to expect, and for several moments, the little girl was quite unable to move.

"I advise you to go quickly," said Miss Day, "for the longer you wait, the worse it will be, I have no doubt."

As the teacher spoke, Elsie heard her father's voice calling her name; struggling to control her fear and trembling, she hurried to obey.

The door to Horace's room was open, and Elsie walked slowly in. "Did you call me, Papa?" she asked.

"Come here to me," he said. He was sitting with her copybook and the report in hand, and she could both see and hear his reproachful attitude. But Horace could see as well, and the terror in Elsie's face touched him. Less sternly he asked, "Can you tell me how it happens that your teacher has brought me so bad a report of your conduct and lessons? She says you have been very idle, and this report tells the same story. Your copybook is really shameful."

Elsie could answer only with tears, which seemed to irritate him. "When I ask a question," he said, "I require an answer at once."

"Oh, Papa. I — I *couldn't* study! I'm very sorry. I'll do better. Please don't be angry with me, Papa!"

"I am angry with you. Very angry, indeed. And strongly inclined to punish you. You couldn't study, eh? For what reason? Were you not well?"

"I don't know, sir."

"You don't know? Well, you could not have been very ill without knowing it, and you seem to have no other excuse. However, I will not punish you this time, as you seem to be truly sorry and have promised to do better. But do not let me see this kind of report again or hear such reports of your

idleness, unless you wish to be severely punished. I warn you, Elsie, that unless your next copybook is much improved, I will certainly punish you."

As he spoke, he leafed through the pages of her writing book. "There are a number of pages here that look quite well done," he noted in a slightly milder tone. "They show what you can do, if you choose. There is an old saying, 'A bird that *can* sing and *won't* sing must be *made* to sing.'"

Elsie started to speak, but he commanded her to be quiet. "Not a word. Just go now." Then he leaned back in his easy chair and began to read his newspaper.

But Elsie, though dismissed, lingered in his room. This was the first time she had ever entered his room, and it should have been a happy occasion. She felt she couldn't leave without some word of kindness from her Papa. But when Horace finally saw her standing there, he only said, "I gave you permission to go, Elsie. Go at once."

So she sought solitude in her own room, and again and again she reproached herself for her failures during the last month. Then she had a thought which added greatly to her misery. Arthur! He was sure to continue his persecutions, and how could she possibly make her copybook more presentable if he would not let her alone? Miss Day usually left the schoolroom during the writing hour, and the older girls were often absent, too. With no one around but the little children, Arthur had ample opportunities to torment her and ruin her work. Elsie didn't tell tales; besides, she could never have sought help from the adults. Arthur was his mother's great favorite, and telling on him would have brought a great deal of trouble to Elsie herself. She wondered if she might persuade her uncle to give her some peace, but that course seemed hopeless.

In desperation, she took her trouble to her Heavenly Father and asked for His help. She was still on her knees when someone knocked on the door. Elsie opened it to find her Aunt Adelaide.

"I'm writing to Rose," Adelaide said cheerfully. "Would you like to write a little note to her? I can enclose it in my letter." But as she spoke, she saw Elsie's tear-stained face and worried expression. "Whatever is the matter, child?" she asked, taking Elsie's hand and drawing her close.

With a great many tears, Elsie sobbed out the whole story, including her father's threat and her fear that she could not, because of Arthur's endless teasing, do well enough to avoid the punishment.

Adelaide's sympathies were fully enlisted, and wiping the child's tears away, she said reassuringly, "Never mind about Arthur, dear. From now on, I will take my book or needlework to the schoolroom every day, and I'll sit there through the writing hour. That will take care of Arthur. But why didn't you tell all this to your father?"

"I don't want to tattle, Aunt Adelaide, and it would make your mother so angry with me. Besides, I can't tell Papa anything."

"I understand," Adelaide comforted, and to herself, she said, "It's no wonder the child can't talk to him. Horace is strangely stern with her, and I mean to give him a good talking to!"

Leaving Elsie with a warm kiss, Adelaide had every intention of finding her brother and carrying out her mission. But he had gone out, and when he returned, brought several gentlemen with him. It was some time before she had the opportunity to get Horace alone, and by then, her resolve had disappeared.

Still, Adelaide's promise had come like an answer to Elsie's prayer, and when her aunt left her room, Elsie's heart was greatly lifted. Locking her door against any surprise intrusion by Enna, Elsie went to her bureau, unlocked a drawer, and removed the purse she was knitting for her father, to replace the one she'd given to Rose Allison. Elsie had started this project even before Horace's return, and now it was nearly finished. How many of her hopes and fears were woven into its bright gold and blue beads!

With her aunt's kind promise fresh in her mind, Elsie settled into her sewing chair and began to work. Her little fingers moved briskly, and the bright, shining needles glanced in and out. As she knitted, her thoughts moved equally swiftly: "No wonder Papa is vexed with me. I've never had such a bad report. What's come over me? It seems I can't study. Maybe I need a holiday. Could it be laziness? If it is, I should be punished. I *will* try harder next month. It's only a month, after all, and then June will be over. Miss Day will go North, and she won't return till August or maybe September, and we'll have a long summer holiday. And this month won't be so hard. No classes on Saturday. That means no class tomorrow, so I can finish this purse. I wonder if Papa will be pleased." She sighed deeply. "I've disappointed him twice this week — the bird and now my bad report. But I will do better next month, especially with Aunt Adelaide's help."

Her thoughts ran on in this way. "I wonder how we will spend our vacation? I went to Ashlands last summer, and then the Carringtons came here, and poor Herbert had such a dreadful time with his hip. How thankful I am not to be lame and always to be so healthy. But Papa probably won't let me go to Ashlands this year, or ask them here. He thinks Lucy isn't a suitable companion, and I was very naughty

when she was here. Have I been more naughty than I ever was before he came home? I wonder if he will punish me severely? I wonder what that means?"

At that, a new and horrible thought struck her, and she dropped her work. "He can't mean *that*! He wouldn't send me away! It would break my heart! I must be very, very good, so that I never deserve a severe punishment; then it makes no difference what he means."

Elsie had heard vague stories about naughty children who were sent away by their parents. She had heard of schools where children actually lived, separated from their families and their homes. In her imagination, this was the most terrible thing that could happen to a child. What if this were the severe punishment her Papa had threatened? The thought of it made her tremble with fear. For all her troubles, she could not bear to be separated from her dear father when she had so recently found him. At the thought of losing him again, she became more determined than ever to do her best to please her Papa and to win his love.

The next day, when she had put the final touches on the beaded purse, she asked Aunt Chloe if her father was at home.

"No, darling," the nurse replied. "He rode out earlier with some gentlemen."

Elsie neatly put away her knitting things and took a piece of notepaper from her desk. Then she wrote, in her very best hand: "A present for my dear Papa, from his little daughter, Elsie." Carefully she pinned the note to the purse and carried it to her father's room. Fearing that he might have returned, she rapped gently at the door, but as there was no answer, she went in. She was about to place the gift on her father's dressing table when his voice startled her.

"What are you doing in my room without my permission?" he demanded.

Elsie quaked and tried to hold back tears as she silently put the purse in his hand. He looked at the present, then at his daughter.

"I made it for you, Papa," she said softly. "Please take it."

"It is really very pretty, " he said, examining the beaded purse closely. "Is this possibly your work? Of course it is. I had no idea you have so much taste and skill. Thank you, Daughter. I'll be happy to take it, and I will use it with great pleasure."

He had taken her hand as he spoke, and now he lifted her onto his knee and asked, "Elsie, my child, why do you always seem so afraid of me? I don't like it."

With a sudden impulse, she threw her arms around his neck and kissed his cheek. Dropping her head onto his shoulder, she sobbed, "Oh, Papa, I love you so very dearly! Won't you love me? I know I've been naughty, but I will try to be good."

For the first time since they had met, Horace folded his child in his arms and kissed her with all the tenderness of a loving parent.

"But I do love you, my little Daughter," he said softly.

So great was Elsie's happiness that she did not try to stop her tears.

"Why are you crying, dear?" Horace asked.

"Because I'm so very happy!"

"Then if you care so much for my love, you mustn't tremble and turn pale whenever I speak to you. I'm not a cruel tyrant, you know."

"It's only because you look so stern. I can't bear to have you so angry with me," she said and added, "but I'm not afraid of you now."

He hugged her again, and as they sat there together, they heard the supper bell. "Now go into my dressing room and wash your face," Horace instructed, "and we'll go down together."

There were several visitors at the table that evening, and the conversation centered on the adults, but every now and then, Horace bestowed a loving look on his daughter, and he carefully attended to all her needs. She was happier than she had ever been.

Things proceeded this way for some time. Elsie did not see as much of her father as she wished, because he was often away on business and he frequently brought guests home on his return. But whenever he saw her, he showed great kindness, and she gradually began to overcome her fear of him. She looked forward to the time when he would have more leisure for her, but she was genuinely happy even so. With her mind now at ease, she could concentrate on her lessons. Adelaide faithfully kept her promise, coming to the schoolroom every day. With Arthur unable to annoy her, Elsie progressed well with her writing; her copybook showed marked improvement in her penmanship. There was not a single blot on any page, and she was actually anticipating with pleasure the next report to her father.

But there came a morning when Miss Day was in her very worst humor — peevish, fretful, irritable, and unreasonable to the extreme. As usual, Elsie took the brunt of her bad temper. Miss Day found fault with everything Elsie did; she scolded and shook the little girl, refused to explain the method of solving a very difficult arithmetic problem, and wouldn't allow the

girl to ask help of anyone else. Then she punished Elsie when the problem was done incorrectly. Elsie struggled to hold back her tears but at last she began to cry, and Miss Day derided her as a baby for shedding tears and a dunce for not understanding the arithmetic.

Elsie bore it all without answering back, but her patience only provoked Miss Day all the more. Finally, when Elsie came up to recite her last lesson, Miss Day deliberately put her questions in the most perplexing way and then didn't allow the child to answer. Throwing down the textbook, Miss Day angrily scolded Elsie and marked down the lesson as a complete failure.

Poor Elsie could take no more. She protested, "I *did* know my lesson Miss Day, every word of it. But you didn't ask your questions as usual or give me time to answer."

"I say you did not know it, and you failed," Miss Day angrily replied. "Now sit down and learn every word of it over again."

But Elsie did not sit down. "I do know it if you will hear me right," she cried indignantly, "and it is unjust of you to mark it a failure."

Miss Day was furious. "Impudent girl!" she screamed. "How dare you contradict me? I'm taking you to your father right now!"

Seizing Elsie by the arm, the teacher dragged her from the room and into the hallway.

"Please don't tell Papa!" Elsie begged, but Miss Day only pushed her to Horace's door. It was open, and he was inside working at his writing desk.

"What is all this?" he asked as they entered.

"Elsie has been very impertinent, sir," Miss Day said. "She accused me of being unjust, and she contradicted me."

Horace was frowning darkly now. "Is this true, Elsie? Did you contradict your teacher?"

"Yes, sir," she said softly.

"Then I certainly must punish you." He picked up a small ruler from his desk and took Elsie's hand as if he meant to strike it.

"Oh, no, Papa!" she cried in alarm. But he put the ruler down and said, "I shall punish you by depriving you of your play today and giving you only bread and water for your dinner." He pointed to a stool in the corner of his large room. "Sit down there and do not move."

Then with a dismissive wave of his hand at Miss Day, he said, "I think she will never do the like again."

Soon after, the dinner bell rang, and Horace left, and after a little time had passed, old Pompey came up the stairs carrying a tray with a tumbler of water and a slice of bread on a plate.

"This isn't much of a meal, Miss Elsie," he said as he put the tray down beside her. "Mr. Dinsmore says it's all you can have, but if you say so, I'll ask Phoebe to send up something more for you before your father comes back."

"That's kind of you, Pompey, but I can't disobey Papa," Elsie said, "and I'm really not hungry at all."

Pompey lingered a bit, hesitant to leave her alone, but Elsie told him to go back to the dining room where he might be needed.

When her father returned, the glass of water and piece of bread lay uneaten on the tray.

"What is the meaning of this?" he demanded. "Why haven't you eaten what I sent to you?"

"I'm not hungry, Papa."

"That's nothing but stubbornness, Elsie, and temper. Take that bread and eat it now. You will eat every crumb and drink every drop of your water."

She obeyed instantly. As he watched, she took a bite of bread, but hard as she tried, she simply could not swallow it. "I can't," she said. "It chokes me."

"You will obey me," he said coldly. "Take some water to wash it down."

She saw that it was no use to protest, and at length every crumb of bread and every drop of water was gone.

His severity in no way diminished, Horace said, "Never dare show me such temper again, Elsie. You won't escape so easily next time. You are to obey me always. Do you understand?"

She knew that his words were unfair — it had not been temper — but Elsie was too fearful now to speak in her own defense. As the tears gathered in her eyes, Horace told her that she was to stay in his room until he returned.

Timidly she asked, "May I have my lesson books, Papa?"

"You may. I'll have them brought to you."

"And my Bible?"

"Yes, yes," he said impatiently as he left the room and shut the door on her.

When he returned to the drawing room, Adelaide asked him what troubled Elsie.

"She has been impertinent to the governess, and I've confined her to my room for the rest of the day," he said with impatience.

"Are you so sure, Horace, that Elsie was to blame?" Adelaide asked as gently as she could. "From what Lora has told me, I believe that Miss Day is often cruelly unfair to your daughter — more than to any of the others."

Horace looked at his sister in surprise. "Are you certain of that?"

"I am. And it is a fact that Miss Day sometimes mistreats her."

Horace colored deeply. "I will not allow that," he said heatedly. But after a moment's thought, he added, "I think you are wrong in this instance, however. Elsie herself acknowledged that she had been impertinent. However severe you think I am, I didn't condemn her without a hearing."

"Believe me, Horace, if she was impertinent, it was after serious provocation. Her acknowledgment is no proof at all, to my mind, for Elsie is so sensitive she'd think herself impertinent simply because Miss Day said so."

"Surely not," he said incredulously. "Elsie does not lack sense."

But Adelaide's words troubled him, and he was half-inclined to go back upstairs and question his child more closely. He considered this, then gave up the idea, telling himself, "If she refuses to be frank with me and speak up for herself, she deserves her punishment. And there was that stubbornness about eating." Horace was very proud, and he did not like to admit, especially to himself, that he may have punished his child unjustly.

It was almost supper time when Horace finally returned to his room, but Elsie didn't hear him enter. He saw that she had not moved from the stool and sat bent over her little Bible. When he came close, she looked up with a start. "Papa," she said, "will you forgive me?"

"Certainly I will, if you are really sorry." He leaned over and kissed her, a cold and dutiful kiss. "Now go let Aunt Chloe dress you for supper."

But Elsie's punishment was not truly over, for she continued to struggle with herself. She was particularly distressed about her bad mark that day and how it would appear on her monthly report. Yet it had not been her fault, and again and again she determined to tell her father what had really happened. Again and again, however, she failed to summon the courage to approach him, and the days passed without her speaking to her father — until it was too late.

Arthur's Scheme

*"For God will bring every deed
into judgment, including
every hidden thing,
whether it is good
or evil."*

ECCLESIASTES 12:14

It was Friday, and Miss Day's reports were to be presented on the next morning. School was over, but Elsie remained alone in the classroom to arrange her books and her writing and drawing materials. When she had finished, she took her report book from the desk and looked over her marks for the last month. As her eye stopped on the one bad mark, she lamented yet again that she had never told her father the whole story of what had occurred. Her copybook, however, gave her complete satisfaction, for every page showed painstaking care and clear improvement. And not a single ink blot marred any of its pages.

"This will surely please Papa," she said to herself. "How good Aunt Adelaide was to come sit with me!"

Then she replaced the copybook and locked her desk securely. She went to her room and placed her desk key in its habitual place on the mantel.

That afternoon, when Elsie and the others had gone out for their walk, Arthur found himself alone in the house with nothing to do. Having gorged himself on candies a few days before, he still felt too sick for his usual activities and lounged lazily in the children's playroom. Although Arthur was not generally fond of reading, he decided to amuse himself with a book he had seen Elsie reading that morning. It was her book, of course, and she was not there to give it to him. But Arthur had very little respect for property rights, except his own.

With Elsie out and Chloe in the kitchen, Arthur felt certain no one would stop him from taking the book, and he

went to Elsie's room. It was lying on the mantel, beside Elsie's desk key. Catching sight of the key, Arthur couldn't suppress a squeal of delight, for he knew exactly which lock the key fit. In an instant, he conceived a plan for the revenge he'd been seeking ever since the affair of his father's gold watch.

His hand reached for the key, but he hesitated. He had to think this through to avoid any chance of detection.

He wanted to deface Elsie's copybook, but Adelaide would testify to the girl's neatness, for his eldest sister had been in the schoolroom every day at writing hour. Adelaide, however, had just left to visit a friend and would be gone from Roselands for several weeks, so she posed no danger. Miss Day, to be sure, well knew the appearance of Elsie's book, but she was even less likely to interfere, and Arthur knew of no one else who could speak up for Elsie.

He decided to run the risk, and he grabbed the key. Checking the hallway to be sure no servants might see him, he hurried to the schoolroom. Almost giddy with glee, he unlocked Elsie's desk and took out her copybook. Using her own pen and ink, he proceeded to blot nearly every page. Some pages got big, black ink drops; others, two or three splatters. He also scribbled between the lines and in the margins so Elsie's work would appear as ugly as possible.

He knew that Horace was sure to be very angry with Elsie, and that thought pleased him mightily, but bad as Arthur was, it must be said that he was unaware of Horace's threatened punishment. The mischief did not take long to accomplish, though Arthur was frightened several times by the sounds of footsteps outside the schoolroom door. No one came in, however, and when the book was thoroughly

ruined, he carefully replaced it, wiped the pen and replaced it too, and locked Elsie's desk. Then he rushed back to Elsie's room, put the key in its place on the mantel, and took the book that had been his original objective.

In all this, he had been seen by no one, and back in the playroom, he settled on a couch to read. But he could think of nothing except his vengeful act and its probable consequences. Now that it was too late, he experienced some doubts; yet he never for a single moment considered confessing and saving Elsie from blame. Then another thought struck him: he had Elsie's book, so it was obvious he had been into her room. That would raise suspicions. He jumped up, intending to take the book back, but at that moment, he heard Elsie's voice from the hall. "Well," he thought to himself, "I'll just bluff it out."

Elsie didn't notice the guilty look on his face when she entered. "I'm looking for the book I was reading. I thought it was in my room," she said, searching likely places. Then she saw it in Arthur's hands. "Oh, you have it! You can keep it, Arthur," she said, "and I'll finish it another time."

But Arthur tossed the book to her. "Take it back," he said roughly. "I don't like it. 'Tisn't any fun."

"I think it's very interesting, and you're welcome to read it," Elsie said politely. "But if you don't want to, I will take it."

The next morning was the last day of the school term, and the writing hour was omitted, so Elsie had no reason to open her copybook. As soon as the children had finished their brief exercises, Miss Day announced, "Young ladies and gentlemen, this is the regular day for your reports, and they

are all prepared. Elsie, here is yours. Now take it and your copybook directly to your father."

Elsie obeyed. She was very conscious of the one bad mark in her report, but her copybook had been written with such care and effort that she hoped her father would not be seriously displeased. Neither she nor anyone else except Arthur knew what had been done to her careful penmanship.

She found her father in his room and handed him the report. With a slight frown, he remarked, "There is one very bad mark here for recitation. But as all the other marks are remarkably good, I will excuse it."

Then he took the copybook. He opened to the first page, and to Elsie's surprise, he threw her a look of great displeasure. His face darkened as he leafed through the rest of the pages. Finally, he said, his voice low and edged with anger, "I see I shall have to keep my promise, Elsie."

"What, Papa?" she asked, turning pale with fear.

"What!" he shouted. "You ask what! Didn't I tell you positively that I would punish you if your copybook did not present a better appearance this month?"

"But it does, Papa! I tried so hard, and there are no blots in it."

"No blots?" He thrust the book under her face. "What do you call these?"

Elsie gazed at the pages of her book in unfeigned astonishment. At first, she could hardly believe the book was really hers. Then she turned to her father and said earnestly, "I didn't do that, Papa."

"Then who did?"

"I don't know, Papa."

"I must get to the bottom of this business," he declared, "and if it isn't your fault, you won't be punished. But if you

are telling a falsehood, Elsie, you shall be punished more severely than if you'd admitted your fault."

Taking her hand, he led her to the classroom where the other children were waiting to meet with their parents. Horace pushed the open copybook at the teacher and asked, "Elsie says these blots are not her work. Can you tell me whose they are?"

"Elsie *generally* tells the truth," Miss Day said smoothly, "but I must say that in this instance, I think she has not. Her desk has a good lock, and she keeps the key, so no one else could have gotten at her copybook."

Horace turned back to his daughter. "Have you ever left your desk unlocked," he asked "or left your key lying about?"

"No, sir, I'm sure I haven't," she answered quickly, though her voice trembled and her face had grown very pale.

"Then I am certain you have told me a falsehood, for the evidence is clear that this must be your work. Come with me." His face was almost as pale as hers, from rage rather than fear, and grabbing her hand again, he dragged her from the room. "I'll teach you to tell the truth to me at least."

Lora, who was just coming back to the schoolroom, heard Horace's angry words. She knew Elsie would never tell a falsehood, and as she looked around the room, her eyes fell on Arthur's guilty face. She hastily crossed to his desk and whispered, "I know that you had a hand in this, Arthur. You'd better confess it quickly, or Horace will half-kill Elsie."

"You don't know anything," Arthur replied.

"Oh, yes, I do," Lora persisted, "and if you don't speak up at once, I will save Elsie myself and find proof of your guilt later. It would be better for you to confess."

Arthur shoved his sister and shouted angrily, "Go away! I have nothing to confess."

Seeing that Arthur could not be moved, Lora rushed to Horace's room and banged the door open without a thought of knocking. She was just in time, for Horace's hand was raised, and he was just about to administer the first spanking of poor Elsie's life. The look he cast at his sister burned with fury, but she took no notice. Instead, Lora cried urgently, "Don't punish Elsie, for I'm sure she's innocent!"

Horace stayed his hand and demanded, "How do you know? What is your proof? Tell me, for I want to be convinced."

Elsie stood rigid at his side, too terrified even to cry.

"In the first place," Lora began, "there is Elsie's established character for truthfulness. In all the time she has been with us, she has always been perfectly truthful in word and deed. And what motive would she have for spoiling her own book? She knew that your punishment was certain to be very severe. Horace, I'm sure Arthur is at the bottom of this. He won't confess, but he doesn't deny it. And I saw Elsie's book just yesterday. It was neat and well written and had absolutely no blots."

Horace's expression changed dramatically as Lora spoke, and he found himself trembling at the thought of what he might have done if his sister had not intervened. "Thank you," he said softly when she finished. "Thank you, dear Lora, for stopping me before I punished Elsie unfairly. I need no more than your word to establish her innocence."

Lora, deeply relieved that she had prevented an injustice, quietly left the room as Horace was taking Elsie into his arms. "My poor child," he said. "My poor little Daughter, I have been terribly unjust to you."

Elsie hardly knew what to reply. "You thought I deserved it, Papa."

"And you have every reason to be angry with me," he continued, his voice strained with emotion. "I love you very much, Elsie, even when I seem cold and stern. And I am more thankful than words can express that I haven't punished you wrongly. I could never forgive myself if I had done that, and I think you have reason now to hate me for what I have done."

This idea struck Elsie like a bolt, and she sobbed, "Oh, Papa, I could never hate you. Never! Never!"

"There, there. Don't cry anymore, dear Daughter," he said, attempting to soothe both her and himself. "Adelaide tells me that perhaps you were not to blame for being impertinent to Miss Day the other day. I want you to tell me all the circumstances now. I won't encourage you to find faults with your teacher, but I also have no intention of allowing you to be mistreated."

"Aunt Lora was there, and she can tell you what happened."

"I want the story from *you*, Elsie. I want to know exactly what passed between you and Miss Day, as best you can remember."

For all her desire to defend herself, Elsie was extremely reluctant to speak against another. She was careful to tell the truth without casting blame on Miss Day, but as she spoke, her father grew increasingly incensed.

"Elsie," he said at last, "if I'd known all this at the time, I would not have punished you. Why didn't you tell me that you were ill treated?"

"But you didn't ask, Papa."

"I asked if it was true that you contradicted Miss Day."

"Yes, sir, and that was true."

"But you should have told me the whole story, though I understand now that I frightened you with my sternness. Well, Daughter," he said gently, "I will endeavor to be less stern in the future, and you must try to be less timid with me."

"I will try, Papa, but I can't help being afraid when you are so angry with me."

Elsie and Horace sat together for a long time, and Elsie talked with him more freely than she had ever done. She spoke about her sorrows and her joys. She told him about Rose Allison and the many happy hours they had spent together in Bible study and prayer. She described how sad she felt when her dear friend went away, and she told him about the wonderful letters she received from Rose. Horace was both pleased by and interested in his child's conversation, and he encouraged her with occasional questions and words of approval. While she was talking, he noticed the gold chain around her neck. "What is this?" he asked.

Gently, Elsie took out the miniature, and Horace needed no explanation to recognize the beautiful face in the portrait. The sight took him back many years, to the few short months he had shared with his wife. Looking from the portrait to his child, he said, as if addressing someone else in the room, "Yes, she is very much like — the same features, the same expression, complexion, hair, and all. She'll be the very counterpart someday."

Elsie caught part of his words, "Am I like Mamma?" she asked him.

"Yes, you are, darling, very much indeed."

"And you loved Mamma?"

"Very dearly."

"Then tell me about her, please," she begged.

"But I haven't much to tell," he sighed. "We knew each other such a short time before we were torn apart. And now we can never meet again on this earth."

"But we may meet her again in heaven, Papa," Elsie said with certainty, "for she loved Jesus, and if we love Him, we will go to heaven when we die. Do you love Jesus, Papa?"

This question greatly concerned Elsie, but instead of answering her, Horace asked, "Do you, Elsie?"

"Oh, yes, sir! Very much. I love Him even better than I love you, my own dear father."

He searched her little face. "How do you know that?" he wondered.

"Just as I know I love you," she responded with evident surprise. "I love to talk of Jesus. I love to tell Him all my troubles, and ask Him to forgive my sins and make me holy. It means so much to know that He loves me and always will, even if no one else does."

Horace set her down from his lap and said, "It's almost dinner time. Go now, and get ready, dear Daughter."

"Are you displeased, Papa?" she asked a little anxiously.

"Not at all, dear," he replied with a gentle laugh. "I thought we might ride together this afternoon. What do you say?"

At her eager response, he again told her to prepare for dinner, but before she could leave, he asked one question more: "Do you remember where you put your desk key yesterday? Did you take it when you went riding?"

"No, sir. I left it on the mantel in my room and —"

She stopped suddenly, but her father instructed her to continue. "I don't want you to express any suspicions," he assured her, "but I must have all the facts you can furnish. Was Aunt Chloe in your room while you were out?"

"No, sir. She was in the kitchen with Aunt Phoebe until I came back."

"Do you know if anyone else entered your room?"

"I don't *know*, sir, but I think Arthur must have been there, because when I came home, he was reading a book I'd left on the mantel."

"Ah, ha!" her father said, and nodded with satisfaction. "Now I see. Elsie, go on to your dinner, and I'll join you shortly."

But Elsie, who did not fully understand the implications of her father's questions, lingered a moment, and when her father looked at her inquiringly, she said, "Please don't be too angry with him, Papa. I don't think Arthur meant to take my book without permission."

"Don't worry, Daughter, I won't hurt him."

It so happened that the elder Mr. Dinsmore and his wife were visiting some friends in the city, and Horace was acting as head of the household in his father's absence. Though Arthur's father was expected back that evening, his mother would be away for several days, and Arthur was beginning to worry very much about the consequences of his actions — not without reason. His brother's wrath was fully aroused, and Horace was determined that this time, his younger brother would not escape punishment for his misdeeds.

Arthur was seated at the table when Horace entered the dining room.

"Step into the library a moment," Horace said to the boy. "I have something to say to you."

Arthur didn't move, but answered back, "I don't want to hear it."

Without raising his voice even a fraction, Horace said, "I'm sure you don't, sir, but that makes no difference. Walk into the library at once."

Under his breath Arthur muttered something about doing as he pleased, but he was too intimidated by Horace's determined look and forceful manner to disobey. Reluctantly he stood up and slowly followed his brother.

In the library, with the door closed, Horace said evenly, "Now tell me how you came to meddle with Elsie's copy-book."

Arthur's denial was hot with false indignation, but Horace simply went on, "It's useless for you to deny it, Arthur, for I know it all. You went to Elsie's room yesterday, when she was out and Aunt Chloe was in the kitchen. You took her desk key from the mantel and went to the school-room and did your mischief, hoping to get her in trouble. When you had returned the key, you thought you had escaped detection. And I very nearly gave my innocent child the spanking you deserve."

Arthur looked up in amazement. "Who told you?" he demanded. "No one saw me!" Then catching himself, he said quickly, "I tell you I didn't do it. I don't know anything about it."

Suddenly, Horace revealed his anger, taking Arthur by the collar and shaking him. "How dare you repeat your falsehood?"

"Let me go," Arthur whined. "I want my dinner."

"You will get no dinner, sir," Horace replied. "I am locking you in your room until our father returns. And if he doesn't punish you as you deserve, I will. I intend that you

receive your just deserts at least once in your miserable life. I know you did this in revenge for the watch business, but I give you fair warning — if you even attempt to harm my child in any way, you will regret it."

Arthur seemed to want to protest, but the look in Horace's eyes told him it was useless. He fell into a sullen whimpering: "You wouldn't treat me like this if Mamma were here."

"But she is not here, and even if she were, she could not save you this time," Horace answered. He had by now hauled Arthur up the stairs and to his bedroom. Horace pushed the boy inside, locked the door, and pocketed the key.

If Arthur expected sympathy from his father, he was sadly disappointed. Mr. Dinsmore took great pride in Horace and trusted his judgment in almost everything. Besides, the older man had a strong sense of justice, and he hated any mean and underhanded behavior. So when the older man returned and Horace had reported on his brother's latest activities, Arthur received a punishment which he truly never forgot.

CHAPTER

9

A Matter of Conscience

"Judge for yourselves whether it is right in God's sight to obey you rather than God."

ACTS 4:19

*H*appy days had come for little Elsie. Her father treated her with the most loving affection and kept her with him as much as possible. He took her wherever he went — riding, walking, on visits to the neighboring plantations. She was much admired for her beauty and sweet disposition, but even with this new attention, she lost none of her natural modesty. She felt grateful for all the kindness she received from others, but her happiest hours were spent at home with her father. She could sit for hours with him, talking or reading. He helped with her studies and taught her some botany and geology on their walks. He helped with her drawing. He sang with her when she played piano, bought her stacks of new sheet music, and hired the best music masters to instruct her. In short, Horace took a lively interest in all she did and gave her the most tender care. He was extremely proud of her, and flattered by the praise of others.

Everyone could see the change in Elsie herself. Her eyes became bright with happiness, and her face lost its pensive expression, becoming as rosy and merry as Enna's.

During their summer holiday, Horace took his daughter traveling, and they stayed at several fashionable resorts. Elsie, who had not traveled anywhere since arriving at Roselands, enjoyed every minute of their trip. They were gone from July until September, and Elsie was rested and ready to resume her studies. But she was not sorry to learn that Miss Day had been delayed in the North for a few weeks and the start of school was to be postponed.

Adelaide was delighted by the changes she saw in Elsie on the day that the child and her father returned home. The family was gathered in the drawing room, and Elsie was entertaining her younger aunts and uncles with stories of her holiday.

"It's good to see how entirely she seems to have overcome her fear of her father," Lora agreed, watching as Elsie ran confidently to Horace and appeared to be asking him for something. With his permission, she displayed a richly bound book of engravings acquired on the journey.

She had, indeed, lost her fear and could now talk to Horace as freely as Enna ever did. And during all their time together, he had never had occasion to scold her or use a single harsh word.

On the first Sabbath afternoon after their return, Elsie was alone in her room. She had asked not to accompany her father on his ride; instead, she spent the time with her favorite books — the Bible, her hymnbook, and *Pilgrim's Progress* — and in self-reflection. She had just opened the Bible to the story of Elijah, which she promised to read to Chloe later, when she heard a rattling at her locked door.

"Open this door right now, Elsie Dinsmore!" Enna shouted imperiously. "I want in!"

Elsie sighed, realizing that this was the end of her nice afternoon, but she opened the door and asked pleasantly, "What do you want, Enna?"

"I want to come in," Enna declared in a saucy little voice, "and I want you to tell me a story. Mamma says you must, because I have a cold and can't go out."

"Well, I'm going to read a beautiful story to Aunt Chloe when she comes back, and you're welcome to stay and listen."

"No!" Enna cried. "I don't want it read." She flounced across the room and took her seat in a delicate rosewood rocking chair that Horace had recently given to his daughter. With her sharp little thumbnail, she began to scratch on the arm of the chair "Please don't do that to my new chair," Elsie said in alarm. "It's a gift from Papa, and I don't want it spoiled."

"Who cares for your old chair," Enna said scornfully and dug another gouge into the wood. "You're a little old maid — so particular about your things. That's what Mamma says. Now, tell me a story."

"If you stop scratching the chair," Elsie said with remarkable patience, "I can tell you about Elijah on Mount Carmel, or Belshazzar's feast, or the children in the fiery furnace. . . ."

"No! None of your old Bible stories. I want to hear the pretty fairy tale that Herbert Carrington likes so much."

"But I can't tell that one today," Elsie said firmly. "I can tell any story that's suitable for the Sabbath and honors God, but not fairy tales. I can tell it to you tomorrow if you wait."

"I want it now!" Enna shouted. "If you don't do what I want, I'll tell Mamma on you!"

With that, the little girl jumped from the chair and dashed out of the room, and it was not many minutes later when a servant came to summon Elsie.

Mrs. Dinsmore began chiding Elsie the moment she walked into her room: "Aren't you ashamed of yourself, Elsie? Why do you refuse Enna so small a favor, especially when the poor child isn't well? I believe you are the most selfish girl I've ever seen."

Elsie tried to explain: "I offered to tell a Bible story or anything suitable for the Sabbath. But it would be wrong to tell a fairy tale today, for the Bible tells us to 'observe the Sabbath day by keeping it holy.'"

"Nonsense! A fairy tale is no more harmful today than any other day," Mrs. Dinsmore said angrily.

At her side, Enna sobbed and whined, "I want a pretty fairy tale. Make her tell me the fairy tale, Mamma!"

Enna's wailing and her mother's scolding had apparently disturbed the elder Mr. Dinsmore, who came charging in from the adjoining room. From his puffy red eyes and tousled hair, Elsie thought he must have been napping, and he was in no mood to listen to a quarrel.

"What's all this fuss?" he roared.

"Nothing," said his wife, whose voice had suddenly grown sweet, "except that Enna is not well enough to go out and wants a fairy tale to help pass the time. And your grand-daughter" — she stared pointedly at Elsie — "is too lazy or willful to tell it."

Mr. Dinsmore turned on Elsie. "Is that so? Well, there's an old saying, little girl. 'A bird that *can* sing and *won't* sing must be *made* to sing.'"

Elsie, who knew the meaning of the saying all too well, started to speak, but Mrs. Dinsmore cut her off. "The child pretends it is all on account of conscientious scruples. She says it isn't fit for the Sabbath. I don't care what that Mrs. Murray taught her. *I* say it is a great impertinence for a child of Elsie's age to set her opinion against yours and mine. I know very well it's just an excuse because she doesn't choose to oblige."

"Of course, it's an excuse," Mr. Dinsmore said hotly. Though by nature a just man, he also had a quick and often unreasonable temper, like all the Dinsmores.

Elsie spoke up, "No, Grandpa. It's not an excuse — "

"How dare you contradict me, you impudent little girl!" Catching her by the arm, he set her down hard on a chair. "Now, little miss," he shouted, "don't move from that chair till your father comes home. Then we'll see what he thinks of such impertinence. If he doesn't give you the punishment you deserve, I miss my guess."

"Please, Grandpa, I — "

Again he stopped her. "Hold your tongue, girl!" he bellowed. "And not another word until your father comes."

For the next half hour — and a very long one it seemed — Elsie sat in silence, wishing for, yet dreading, her father's return. Would he punish her as her grandfather seemed to wish? Or would he listen patiently to her side of the story? Might she be punished in either case? A few months before, she would have been certain of serious chastisement. And even now, though she trusted her father's love beyond a doubt, she also knew that Horace was a strict disciplinarian who never excused her faults.

At last she heard the sound of his steps in the hall, and her heart beat faster as he entered the room and addressed his father, "You wanted to see me, sir?"

"I want you to attend to this girl," Mr. Dinsmore said gruffly, nodding his head toward Elsie. "She has been very impertinent to me."

Horace's expression was of complete amazement, and he turned to her with such grave eyes that her tears immediately began to flow.

"It is hard to believe," Horace said, "that my little Elsie could be guilty of such conduct. If she has been, she must be punished, for I cannot allow this kind of behavior. Elsie, go to my dressing room and stay there until I come to you."

"Papa, I — "

"Hush!" he commanded with some of the old sternness. Sobbing, Elsie instantly obeyed.

Horace took a seat and turned to his father. "Now, sir, if you please, I'd like to hear the whole story," he said calmly. "Precisely what has Elsie done and said? What was the provocation, for that must be taken into account if I am to do her justice."

"If you do her justice, you'll spank her well," Mr. Dinsmore grumbled.

Horace colored deeply, for he strongly resented interference in his management of his child. But he calmed himself and asked again for the details. Mr. Dinsmore deferred to his wife, and she painted as bleak a picture as she could against Elsie. She was, however, obliged to state that it was Elsie's refusal to humor Enna and to tell a fairy story on the Sabbath that started the whole upset. This admission vexed Horace immensely, and he informed his stepmother that, while he did not always approve of Elsie's strict notions on such matters, his daughter was not to be made a slave to Enna's whims. If Elsie chose to tell Enna a story — or do anything for her — he had no objection. But never was Elsie to be forced, and Enna must understand that she had no right to Elsie's favors.

His father, hearing the whole story for the first time, agreed.

"You are right there, Horace," he said, "but that doesn't excuse Elsie's impertinence to me. I have to agree with my wife that it is a great piece of impudence to set her opinions against ours. Besides, she contradicted me flatly."

He then related the exact words of his exchange with Elsie. But he changed the tone of her words, and omitted the fact that he had interrupted her before she could complete a

sentence. From this recounting, Horace received the erroneous impression that Elsie had been very disrespectful, and he left the room with every intention of giving her a severe punishment indeed. But as he walked slowly to his room, his anger began to cool, and he determined that, to be fair, he must hear her side of the story before he condemned her.

When he entered his room, Elsie could see that his face was sad and serious, but there was little sternness in it. He sat beside her on the couch and hugged her gently. Finally, he said, "I am very sorry to hear so bad an account of your behavior. I don't want to punish you."

Elsie didn't say anything, but he could feel her shaking as she cried.

"I won't condemn you unheard," he said gently. "Now tell me how you came to be impertinent to your grandfather."

"I didn't mean to be saucy," she managed to say.

"Then stop crying and tell me everything that happened. I want to know what words passed between you and Enna, as well as Mrs. Dinsmore and your grandfather. I know I can trust you to tell the truth and not to use a falsehood to save yourself from punishment."

"Thank you for saying that, Papa," Elsie said, smiling up at him. "I will try to tell you just what happened."

Carefully, she repeated everything that had occurred, word-for-word when she could. Her account sounded very different from her grandfather's, and she added that she had tried to explain to Mr. Dinsmore that it was not unwillingness to oblige Enna, but fear of doing wrong that led her to refuse to tell the fairy story.

"Was I very naughty?" she asked when she had finished.

"So much depends on the tone," her father said honestly. "If you spoke to your grandfather as you did in repeating

your words just now, then no, I don't think you were impertinent. But you must always treat your grandfather with respect. And understand that to him there is something quite unseemly about a little girl setting her opinion against that of her elders. You must never do that with me."

Elsie hung her head and asked, "Are you going to punish me, Papa?"

"Yes," he said, "but first I'm going to take you downstairs to ask your grandfather's pardon. I know you don't want to do it, but you must."

"I'll do whatever you want, Papa, but please tell me what to say."

"You must say 'Grandpa, I did not intend to be disrespectful, and I'm very sorry for whatever seemed impertinent in my words or tones. Will you please forgive me, and I will try always to be respectful in the future.' You can say all of that with truth, can't you?"

"Yes sir, because I am sorry and I do intend to be respectful to Grandpa always."

When they went to his father's room, Horace said, "Elsie has come to beg your pardon, sir."

Mr. Dinsmore, casting a triumphant look at his wife, said, "That's as it should be. I told the girl you wouldn't support any such impertinence."

"I will never support her in wrongdoing," Horace replied, a marked tone of displeasure in his voice, "but neither will I allow her to be imposed upon. Now speak, Elsie, what I told you to say."

When Elsie had sobbed out her apology, Mr. Dinsmore said coldly, "Yes, I must forgive you, girl, but I hope your father won't let you off without a proper punishment."

"I will attend to that," Horace replied in a tone as frosty as his father's. "I certainly intend to punish her *as she deserves*."

He had laid special stress on those final words, and Elsie totally misunderstood his meaning. She trembled so with fear that he had to carry her back to his room. When they were out of anyone's hearing, he wiped her tears away and said with a smile, "Don't be so afraid, Elsie. I'm not going to be severe."

She looked at him in glad surprise.

"I said I would punish you as you deserve, so I intend to keep you here with me until your bedtime. You can't go down to supper, and I'm going to give you a long lesson that you must be able to recite perfectly before you go to bed."

Elsie worried for a moment that the lesson might be something inappropriate for the Sabbath, but she relaxed when her father took his Bible and pointed to the thirteenth and fourteenth chapters of John.

"But that won't be a real punishment, Papa," she laughed. "I love these chapters, and I've read them so often I almost know all the words already."

Pretending to be very stern, Horace said, "Hush! Don't tell me my punishments are *no* punishments. Now take your book to that seat by the window and learn what I tell you."

Horace took up a newspaper, but in fact he spent most of his time looking at his child as she diligently studied the holy book. It struck him with great force how important she was to him, and he wondered how he could ever have been harsh with her.

When the supper bell rang, Horace got up to leave. "I'll send some supper up to you, and I want you to eat it," he said at the door.

"Will it be bread and water, Papa?" she asked with a smile.

"Wait and see," he laughed.

~~~~~

The tray of food that Pompey soon brought to Elsie was a far cry from the fare provided during her last imprisonment. Elsie was truly astonished when she saw a plate of hot, buttered muffins, a large piece of broiled chicken, a cup of jelly, and another cup filled to the brim with steaming coffee.

"I reckon you have been a very nice girl today," Pompey said as he set the tray down, "or else your Papa thinks you're a little sick."

As Elsie put away her book and began to eat, Pompey told her, "Just ring the bell if you want something more, and I'll fetch it for you. Your father told me so himself."

Elsie certainly enjoyed every crumb of her supper, and when Horace returned, she thanked him graciously. "But I thought you didn't allow me such things," she commented.

Playfully, he said, "Don't you know, Daughter, that I am absolute monarch of this small kingdom and you are not to question my decrees?"

His tone then became more serious, "I do not allow it as a rule, because I do not think it for your good. But this once, I don't think it will hurt. I know that you don't presume on favors, Elsie, and I wanted to indulge you a bit. I think you were made to suffer more than you deserved this afternoon."

His words were very tender, and before he went on, he kissed her gently on the forehead.

"Don't think, though, that I'm excusing you for imperti-nence. I am not. But what you had to endure from Enna's insolence — it will stop, for I will not have it."

"I don't mind it much, Papa," Elsie responded. "I'm used to it, for Enna has always treated me that way."

"And why did I never hear this before?" he asked, his tem-per rising. "It's abominable! Not to be endured! And I shall see that Miss Enna is made to understand that *my* daughter is fully her equal in every respect and to be treated as such."

Elsie, who was somewhat frightened at his vehemence, made no reply, and her father continued in a somewhat softer tone, "I have no doubt your grandfather and his wife would have liked me to force you to give in to Enna's whim. But you are to use your own judgment wherever Enna is concerned. If I had bidden you to tell her that story, well, that would have been a different matter. You are never to set your will, or your opinion of right and wrong, against mine, Elsie, for I won't allow it. I don't altogether like some of these strict notions of yours, and I give you fair warning — should they ever come into conflict with my wishes and commands, you are to give them up.

"But don't look so alarmed, Elsie," he added very kindly. "I hope that will never happen."

Her face was very serious as she lay her hand on his shoulder and said, "Oh, Papa! Please don't ever ask me to do anything wrong. It would break my heart."

"Elsie dear, I never want you to do wrong. On the con-trary, I want you always to do right. But *I* must be the judge of what is right and wrong for you. Remember that you are only a little girl and not yet capable of judging for yourself. As long as you obey your father without hesitation, there will be no problem."

His tone was kind but firm, and Elsie had a strange sense as he spoke, as if she were in the shadow of some great, impending trouble. But with some effort, she managed to banish this feeling of foreboding and enjoy her present blessings. She knew that her father loved her dearly, and he was not requiring her to do anything against her conscience. Perhaps he never would. God could incline his heart to respect her principles. Or if the dreaded trial should happen, He would give her His wisdom and strength to bear it, for she remembered His promise, "And God is faithful; He will not let you be tempted beyond what you can bear. But when you are tempted, He will also provide a way out so that you can stand up under it."

"What are you thinking about?" Horace asked her at length.

"A good many things, Papa. I was thinking of what you said and how glad I am to know that you truly love me. And I was asking God to help us both to do His will. And I thought that I might be able to always do what you bid, without disobeying Him. May I say my lesson now? I think I know it perfectly."

"Of course," he said in an abstracted way.

Elsie brought the Bible to him and drew up a stool for herself beside his chair. With her arm over his knee, she began to repeat with great feeling the chapters she had learned — the touching description of the Last Supper and Jesus' farewell to His sorrowing disciples.

"Isn't it beautiful, Papa?" she asked when she had finished her recitation. "'Having loved His own who were in the world, he now showed them the full extent of His love,'" she quoted again.

"It seems so strange that Jesus could be so thoughtful of them when all the time He knew the dreadful death He was going to die. And He knew they were all going to run away and leave Him to His enemies. It's so sweet to know that Jesus is so loving and that He loves me and will love me forever."

"But do you think you are good enough for Jesus to love you?" Horace asked.

"I know I'm not at all good, Papa," she said with grave seriousness. "My thoughts and feelings are often wrong, and Jesus knows all about it. But that doesn't keep Him from loving me because it was sinners He died to save. How good and kind He is. And who could help loving Him?"

She looked up into her father's eyes, and Horace was surprised to see sadness there as she went on, "I used to feel so lonely sometimes, Papa, that I thought my heart would really break. I think I would have died if I had not had Jesus to love me."

Her words moved Horace deeply, and he asked, "When were you so lonely and sad, darling?"

"Sometimes when you were away and I'd never seen you, I used to think of you and my heart would ache to see you and have you hold me and call me Daughter, as you do now." She paused and had to struggle to keep back her tears. Then she said, "But when you came home, Papa, and I saw you didn't love me — oh, that was the worst. I just wanted to die and go to Jesus and to Mamma."

She broke into tears, and Horace lifted her to his lap, hugging her close. "It was very, very cruel of me," he said, his own voice choking with emotion. "I don't know how I could close my heart like that. But I had been much prejudiced and led to believe that you feared and disliked me as a cruel tyrant."

Elsie was amazed at this admission. "How could you think that, Papa? I've *always* loved you, ever since I can remember."

Later, in her own room, Elsie thought seriously of everything that had happened that day and everything her father had said. In her prayers, she expressed many thanks to the Lord that her father had learned to love her. Then she added a fervent petition that her father would come to love Jesus and would never bid her to break any of God's commands. But the gray shadow of foreboding had not vanished entirely, and storm clouds were already gathering in the distance.

CHAPTER

10

Elsie's Sabbath Day Choice

*"If you keep your feet from breaking the Sabbath
and from doing as you please on my holy day,
if you call the Sabbath a delight and the
Lord's holy day honorable, and if you
honor it by not going your own way
and not doing as you please or
speaking idle words, then you will
find your joy in the Lord...."*

ISAIAH 58:13–14

On a Sabbath day some weeks later, quite a few guests had dined at Roselands and were gathered in the drawing room. The gentlemen were laughing and joking, talking of politics, and conversing with the ladies, and everyone was in high spirits.

Adelaide, noticing that one of the men was glancing about the room in an attitude of disappointment, said, "May I ask what you are searching for, Mr. Eversham?"

"Yes, Miss Adelaide. I was looking for little Elsie. Edward Travilla has given me such a glowing account of her musical talent that I hoped to hear her sing and play."

"And so you shall, Eversham," said Horace, who had overheard his guest's request. He crossed the room to summon a servant, but he was stopped by a hand on his arm.

"You'd better not send for her," Mrs. Dinsmore whispered.

"May I ask why not?" he inquired in a tone of annoyance.

"Because she will not sing," his stepmother replied coolly.

"Pardon me, madam, but I think she will, if I bid it."

Though Horace was becoming heated at the woman's words, Mrs. Dinsmore maintained her cool, haughty manner as she said, "No, she will not. She will tell you she is wiser than her father and that it will be a sin to obey you. Believe me, Horace, she will defy your authority. You had

better take my advice and leave her alone. Save yourself from the embarrassment."

Horace, biting his lip to control his anger, replied, "Thank you, madam, but I believe this lies solely in your imagination. I'm at a loss to understand you, for Elsie has never shown the slightest resistance to my authority."

With a slight arch of her eyebrow, Mrs. Dinsmore left him, and Horace gave the bell rope a hard pull. A servant appeared and was sent to summon Elsie. Horace joined a group around the piano, where Adelaide had just begun to play.

Though outwardly calm, Horace was already having doubts about his action. He had never understood the full depth of his child's convictions, and in his desire to display Elsie's talents, he had forgotten her conscientious scruples about the observance of the Sabbath. But he saw clearly that there would be a struggle, for on a point of principle, Elsie would be as unyielding as he. Though he felt sure Elsie would obey him in the end, he might have avoided the conflict but for his pride. He had gone too far to retreat, and perhaps, he told himself, it was just as well that this inevitable struggle should take place here and now.

When the servant came to her room with her father's message, Elsie immediately sensed what was about to occur. Elsie had been taught since her earliest days that the Sabbath is a day to rest and honor God by focusing on Him. With alarm now, she said to herself, "Papa wants me to do something that is not right on the Sabbath." Though she hoped that she was wrong, she nevertheless knelt quickly and prayed to the Lord for the strength to do right.

When she entered the drawing room, her father greeted her affectionately, but Elsie turned pale as he led her to the piano where Adelaide had just finished playing. He selected a piece of music that Elsie had learned during their holiday and handed it to her. "My friends are anxious to hear you play and sing," he said, "and I think this song will be perfect."

In almost a whisper, she said, "Won't tomorrow do, Papa?"

From the corner of his eye, Horace caught the smug expression of Mrs. Dinsmore as he replied to Elsie, "Certainly not, Daughter. You know this piece very well without more practice."

"That's not the reason," the little girl said. "But you know today is the holy Sabbath."

"What of it, child?" he asked, struggling to keep his voice mild. "I consider this song perfectly proper to be sung today. That should satisfy you that you are not doing wrong. Remember what I told you a few weeks ago. Now, sit down and sing."

"Oh, Papa, I can't sing it today! Please let me wait until tomorrow!"

But in his most stern manner, Horace commanded Elsie to sit and perform. She complied to the extent of taking the stool, but with her eyes full of tears, she again refused to sing. "I can't, Papa! I can't break the Sabbath," she cried in heartfelt agony.

"You must," he said as he placed the music before her. "I've told you it will not be breaking the Sabbath, and you must let me be the judge."

At this point, several of the guests urged Horace to let the matter go. Adelaide good-naturedly said, "Let me play it, Horace. I think I can do it almost as well as Elsie."

Horace could not be swayed. "I have given my child a command, and it must be obeyed," he said sternly. "She may not set her opinion of right and wrong against mine."

But Elsie, tears streaming down her face, made no move to obey her father. An uncomfortable silence settled on everyone for a few moments, until Horace finally said, "You shall sit here until you obey me, Elsie, no matter how long it takes."

"Yes, Papa," she replied, her words barely audible, and with relief, the guests drifted away from the scene.

Horace went to join a group of the men when Mrs. Dinsmore halted him with a remark. "I told you," she said in a low, self-satisfied tone, "how it would end."

"But it hasn't ended," Horace snapped, "and before it does, Elsie will know who has the stronger will."

Though none of the guests talked to her, Elsie felt that they were all looking at her, and the embarrassment was hard to bear. She was deeply troubled, too, by the thought that her father's displeasure would lead to the withdrawal of his affection entirely. As the time passed, she became extremely uncomfortable on the little seat of the music stool. It was an unusually warm fall afternoon, and the sultry heat of the drawing room caused her head to throb. Feeling that she might faint, she leaned forward and rested her head on the piano.

She had sat this way for almost two hours, when Edward Travilla came to her side. "I'm so sorry for you, my little friend," he said gently, "but I advise you to submit to your father. You can never conquer him, for I've never known a more determined man. Won't you sing the song? It will only take a few minutes, and your trouble will be over."

Elsie raised her tear-stained face. "But, Mr. Travilla, I don't want to conquer my father," she said earnestly. "I want to obey him in everything and honor him as the Bible tells me. But I can't disobey God, even to please my Papa."

"But, Elsie, would it really be disobeying God? Is there any verse in the Bible that says you must not sing songs on Sunday?"

"The Bible says to keep the Sabbath *holy*. It says that we are not to do as we please or go our own way or speak idle words. We're to rest from our work and honor God by giving all our attention to Him. We're to study the Bible, or worship and praise Him. But, Mr. Travilla, there's not a word of praise in that song. Not one word about God or heaven. I wish it were a song of praise; then I could obey my father."

Seeing that he could not convince the child, in spite of her obvious desire to please her father, Edward approached his friend. "Horace," he said, "I'm convinced that Elsie is entirely conscientious. Won't you give in to her in this instance?"

"Never!" Horace replied with some consternation. "This is the first time she has rebelled against my authority, and if she succeeds, she will expect to have her way always. I must subdue her now, whatever the cost."

The elder Mr. Dinsmore added his hearty agreement. "Quite right," he said. "Let her know from the start that you are the master."

"But I have to question a parent's right to coerce a child to act against her conscience," Edward contended, then added in a lowered voice. "You know, my friend, that this is no rebellion against you but entirely a matter of faith."

"Nonsense!" Horace replied harshly, but in truth this battle of wills with his daughter was wearing him down

191

almost as much as his poor child. "Elsie must learn to let me be the judge in these matters for many years to come."

Edward Travilla was not the only guest discomforted by Horace's strong discipline. At the moment, Mr. Eversham, who was feeling regret and responsibility for what had happened, was asking Adelaide if she might tell him how to repair the situation. But Adelaide could only shake her head sadly. "There's no moving my brother," she said, "and as for Elsie, I doubt any power on earth can make her do what she considers wrong."

"But where did she get such odd notions?" Eversham asked.

"Partly from the Scottish lady who cared for her for many years," Adelaide explained, "and partly from her Bible study. She is forever reading her Bible. I think it would break the child's heart to do anything that she sincerely believes would betray her faith."

"Then I can do nothing," Mr. Eversham said with a sigh.

Another hour dragged by, and when the supper bell rang, Horace went to his daughter and asked her once more to sing the song. She again refused.

"Very well," he said in a voice that no longer held any anger. "You know I cannot break my word. You must stay here until you obey, and you cannot eat until you do. Your obstinacy is causing great pain for us both."

After supper, the guests moved to the veranda where the breeze was cool, and Elsie was left alone in the darkening drawing room. The air inside the room seemed to draw close around her, and at times she could barely get her breath. Her whole body ached, and the pain pounded in her head. Her thoughts began to wander, and she forgot where she was. Her head seemed to spin, and everything swirled in confusion until she finally lost all consciousness.

Horace, Edward, and several others were talking just outside the drawing room when a sudden noise as of something falling startled them. Edward rushed inside, and seeing a small bundle by the piano, he rushed to Elsie.

"A light, quick!" he shouted as he raised the child. "She's fainted."

One of the men found a lamp and brought it close. In the light, they could see Elsie's deathly pale face and a stream of blood from a gash on her temple. She was a pitiable sight — her hair, face, and neat white dress covered with blood.

"Horace, you're a brute!" Edward said as he gently laid the child on a sofa. Horace bent over his little girl, but he was too anguished to make a reply.

Fortunately, there was a physician among the guests, and he hurried to treat Elsie's wound and give her restoring medication. But it was some time before she returned to consciousness, and her father was all this while terrified that she might die. But when her eyes at last opened, she gazed at Horace and asked, "Are you angry with me, Papa?"

"No, no, my darling child," he murmured. "Not at all."

"But what happened?" she asked in bewilderment. "What did I do?"

"Not a thing," he assured. "You were ill, but you are better now, so don't think any more about it."

The doctor said Elsie should be put to bed at once, and Horace tenderly cradled her in his arms and carried her upstairs.

"There's blood on my dress, Papa," Elsie said weakly.

"You fell and hurt your head, but you will be fine now."

"Oh! I remember," she moaned.

Horace helped Chloe, who was steady as a rock even at the sight of so much blood, and they prepared Elsie for bed.

"Are you hungry, darling?" Horace asked.

"No, Papa, I just want to sleep."

So Horace carried her to the bed and was about to tuck her in when Elsie suddenly cried, "My prayers, Papa!"

"Not tonight, dear. You're too weak."

"Please, Papa. I can't sleep otherwise."

So he helped her to her knees and listened as she spoke. To his surprise, he heard his own name mentioned more than once, coupled with a request that he should come to love Jesus.

When Elsie was at last wrapped in her covers, he asked, "Why did you pray that I might love Jesus?"

"Because I want you to be happy, and I want you to go to heaven, Papa."

"And what makes you think I don't love Him?"

"Don't be angry, Papa, but you know what Jesus says: 'Whoever has my commands and obeys them, he is the one who loves me.'" As Horace leaned down to kiss her good night, Elsie threw her arms around his neck and whispered, "I love you very, very much."

"Better than anyone else?" he asked with a smile.

"I love Jesus best, and you next."

When she woke the next morning, Elsie felt nearly as good as ever. After her bath, Chloe carefully brushed her hair so the curls concealed the bandage on her temple, and except for a slight paleness, there was nothing about Elsie's appearance to betray the accident.

She was reading her morning Bible chapter when her father came in and sat down beside her. "You look very pretty this morning," he said, winning a sweet smile. "How do you feel?"

"Fine, Papa."

"Do you know that you came very near dying last night?"

Elsie's face showed obvious disbelief, and Horace explained, in a voice that trembled with emotion, "The doctor says that if the wound had been half an inch nearer your eye. . . . Well, I might have lost my little girl."

Elsie said nothing for a few moments, then she asked, very softly, "Would you have been very sorry?"

"Oh, Elsie," he said, almost overcome by her question. "You are more precious to me than all my wealth, all my friends, and all my family. I would rather part with everything else than lose you."

She lapsed into silence again until he inquired what was on her mind now.

"I was just wondering whether I was ready to go to heaven, Papa. I think I was. I know I love Jesus, and I know Mamma would be glad to see me. Don't you think she would?"

"I can't spare you yet," he said, trying to keep his emotions under control, "and I think she loves me too well to wish it, dearest child."

Elsie continued to consider these things solemnly that morning, and as there was no school and her father was called into a business discussion, she retreated to the garden to read her Bible. She had been alone there for some time when she heard someone approaching. It was Edward Travilla.

He saw how intent she looked, and sitting beside her, he glanced at the book she held.

"What can you be reading that affects you so?" he asked.

"Oh, Mr. Travilla, doesn't it make your heart ache to read how our dear Savior was so abused, and then to know it was all because of our sins. Isn't it wonderful to know that we can be saved from the penalty for our sins, and be His friend now, and someday go to heaven?"

Her ideas intrigued him. "Really, Elsie," he said, "you are quite right, but aren't such ideas very serious for a young girl like you?"

"Mr. Travilla," she exclaimed. "These ideas bring me such peace and joy. When I read my Bible like this, I sometimes feel as if Jesus were sitting here beside me, just as you are."

"Can a person really be that close to God?" he asked half-jokingly.

"Oh yes, sir. Our dear Savior wants all His children to draw near to Him. You only have to *want* to spend time with Him, for He is always ready and waiting with His love," she replied.

"And how did you come to have such a close relationship with Jesus?"

"Aunt Chloe and Mrs. Murray taught me from the Bible, Mr. Travilla, that everyone who calls on the name of the Lord will be saved. I was just a little girl when I asked Him to forgive my sins and come into my heart."

"Then perhaps you know these words," he said and quoted, "'For God so loved the world that He gave His one and only Son, that whoever believes in Him shall not perish but have eternal life. For God did not send His Son into the world to condemn the world, but to save the world through Him.'"

Elsie nodded, for she knew the verses well.

Edward, who found himself curious about the depth of the child's faith, went on, "Do you think it is necessary for a person to ask in order to be saved, my little friend? What of a person who simply leads an honest, upright, and moral life? Cannot that person be saved?"

Elsie thought for several moments, then said slowly, "I know that the Bible teaches that there is not a person on earth who always does right and never sins. The Bible says it is by *grace* that we are saved, through our faith in Jesus — not by our good deeds. I don't think we could ever be perfect enough to win God's love and forgiveness. But we don't have to be perfect, because God gives us His gifts freely. The Bible says that we only have to believe with our hearts and confess with our mouths that Jesus Christ is Lord, that He died for our sins and rose from the dead. Do you remember, Mr. Travilla, that the Bible tells us that to enter the Kingdom of God we must be 'born again'?"

"And do you know what is meant by being born again?"

"It means that when we accept Jesus' death on the cross as payment for our sins," Elsie explained as carefully as she could, "then God's Holy Spirit comes to live in us and changes our hearts. We are born into a new life. That's the life of the Spirit, Mr. Travilla. And our change of heart makes us want to honor Jesus and be like Him and please Him in every way — not because we have to, but because we love Him and *want* to do it."

As Edward looked into Elsie's solemn little face, he suddenly remembered something else Jesus had said: "I praise you, Father, Lord of heaven and earth, because you have hidden these things from the wise and learned, and revealed them to little children." It was now obvious to Edward that the child had been very well taught, but he marveled that

her acceptance of these great Bible truths was so natural. "No wonder," he thought to himself, "that Jesus spoke of the need to have 'faith as a little child.'"

Suddenly Edward saw tears welling in Elsie's bright eyes, and in an attempt to jolly her out of this serious mood, he said teasingly, "Well, my little friend, let us hope that everyone will repent and believe before they die."

But Elsie heard nothing humorous in his comment. She looked at him and asked, "Do you know how near I came to death last night? Then you know there can never be time enough, Mr. Travilla."

Edward, still wondering at this child's unusual spiritual maturity, quoted, more to himself than his little companion, "Blessed are the pure in heart for they shall see God."

Realizing that the morning was almost over and they would soon be expected for dinner, Edward hurriedly walked Elsie back to the house where the guests were gathered in the drawing room. When Horace saw his daughter enter the room, he asked her to sing, and Elsie obliged with enthusiasm. Her performance made her father very proud indeed.

For all his outward reserve, the events of the previous day had greatly deepened Horace's tender feelings for his daughter. His one desire now was to protect her from all dangers and to save her from the unhappiness of so many children who were raised without discipline. His own brother Arthur, not yet in his teens, was already a liar and a sneak. Horace would never let such a fate befall his beloved child. In their short time together, she had become more important to him than his own life.

Looking into Elsie's lovely face, so much like his lost wife's, he wondered how he could ever have been prejudiced

against her or doubted her love for him. One thing he would never forget, and that was how close he had been to losing his precious little Elsie forever.

As Elsie began to sing another cheerful song for her father, Edward, standing somewhat apart from the group around the piano, regarded his old friend closely. Although he often disagreed with Horace's stern methods, he knew that Horace only wanted what was best for the child and had come to love Elsie as much as she loved him.

"But his love may not be enough," Edward thought, "for I fear Horace still does not share the deeper love that is Elsie's first loyalty. Can he ever understand how God's love sustained her through all those lonely years when her earthly father was absent? I wonder what their future will be. Can their happiness survive another clash between Horace's pride and Elsie's faith?"

Edward was so deep in his musings that he failed to notice when Adelaide came to stand at his side.

"Why, Mr. Travilla," she said brightly, "what makes you look so gloomy on this happy day?"

Quickly recalling himself to the present, Edward replied with a smile, "Not gloomy at all, Miss Dinsmore. It is only that the sight of your brother and your niece reminded me of some words of Scripture I learned many years ago."

Adelaide followed Edward's gaze to Elsie's shining face. "And will you share those words with me, Mr. Travilla?" she asked.

Edward began to speak with an intensity that surprised Adelaide. "'Let the little children come to me,'" he quoted, "'and do not hinder them, for the Kingdom of God belongs to such as these.'"

Are Elsie's troubles *really* over?
Will her father *ever* understand her and the deep faith that guides her?
Can she find love at Roselands?

Elsie's story continues in:

ELSIE'S IMPOSSIBLE CHOICE

Book Two of the
*A Life of Faith:
Elsie Dinsmore* Series

Available at your local bookstore

Collect all of our Elsie Dinsmore books and companion products!

Check out
www.alifeoffaith.com

 Get news about Elsie and her cousin Millie and other *A Life of Faith* characters

 Find out more about the 19th century world they live in

 Learn to live a life of faith like they do

 Learn how they overcome the difficulties we all face in life

Find out about *A Life of Faith* products

Join our girls' club

A Life of Faith: Elsie Dinsmore
"It's Like Having a Best Friend From Another Time"

Collect all of our Millie products!

A Life of Faith: Millie Keith Series

* Now Available as a Dramatized Audiobook!

Collect all of our Violet products!

A Life of Faith: Violet Travilla Series

Mission City Press

For more information, write to

Mission City Press at 202 Seond Ave. South,
Franklin, Tennessee 37064
or visit our Web Site at:

www.alifeoffaith.com

— ABOUT THE AUTHOR —

*M*artha Finley was born on April 26, 1828, in Chillicothe, Ohio. Her mother died when Martha was quite young, and her father, James Finley, a doctor and devout Christian, soon remarried. Martha's stepmother, Mary Finley, was a kind and caring woman who always nurtured Martha's desire to learn and supported her ambition to become a writer.

Martha was well-educated for a girl of her times. After her father's death in 1851, she began her teaching career in Indiana. She later lived with an elder sister in New York City, where Martha continued teaching and began writing stories for Sunday school children. Martha also lived in Philadelphia where her early stories were first published by the Presbyterian Publication Board, and then she worked as a teacher in Phoenixville, Pennsylvania for two years. Determined to become a full-time writer, Martha returned to Philadelphia. Even though she sold several stories (some written under the pen name of "Martha Farquharson"), her first efforts at novel-writing were not successful. But during a period of recuperation from a fall, she crafted the basics of a book that would make her one of the country's best-known and most beloved novelists.

Three years after Martha began writing Elsie Dinsmore, the story of the lonely little Southern girl was accepted by the New York firm of Dodd Mead. The publishers divided the original manuscript into two complete books; they also honored Martha's request that pansies (flowers, Martha explained, that symbolized "thoughts of you") be printed on the books' covers. Released in 1868, Elsie Dinsmore became the publisher's best-selling book that year, launching a series that sold millions of copies at home and abroad.

The Elsie stories eventually expanded to twenty-eight volumes and included the lives of Elsie's children and grandchildren. Miss Finley published her final Elsie novel in 1905. Four years later, she died less than three months before her eighty-second birthday. She is buried in Elkton, Maryland, where she lived for more than thirty years in the house she built with proceeds from her writing career. Her large estate, carefully managed by her youngest brother, Charles, was left to family members and charities.

Martha Finley was a remarkable woman who lived a quiet Christian life; yet through her many writings, she affected the lives of several generations of Americans for the better. She never married, never had children, yet she left behind a unique legacy of faith.

A LIFE OF FAITH®

Girls Club

An Imaginative New Approach to Faith Education

*I*magine…an easy way to gather the young girls in your community for fun, fellowship, and faith-inspiring lessons that will further their personal relationship with our Lord, Jesus Christ. Now you can, simply by hosting an A Life of Faith Girls Club.

This popular Girls Club was created to teach girls to live a *lifestyle* of faith.

Through the captivating, Christ-centered, historical fiction stories of Elsie Dinsmore, Millie Keith, Violet Travilla, and Laylie Colbert, each Club member will come to understand God's love for her, and will learn how to deal with timeless issues all girls face, such as bearing rejection, resisting temptation, overcoming fear, forgiving when it hurts, standing up for what's right, etc. The fun-filled Club meetings include skits and dramas, application-oriented discussion, themed crafts and snacks, fellowship and prayer. What's more, the Club has everything from official membership cards to a Club Motto and original Theme Song!
